THE
BIGFOOT
GANG

E.D.G. SMITH

The Bigfoot Gang
Copyright © 2016 by EDG Smith. All rights reserved.
First Edition: December 2017

No part of this book may be reproduced, scanned, or distributed in any printed or electronic form without permission. Please do not participate in or encourage piracy of copyrighted materials in violation of the author's rights. Thank you for respecting the hard work of this author.

This is a work of fiction. Names, characters, places, and incidents either are the product of the author's imagination or are used fictitiously, and any resemblance to locales, events, business establishments, or actual persons—living or dead—is entirely coincidental.

Connect with the author at:
www.edgsmith.com
www.facebook.com/edgsmith

Manufactured in the United States of America.

ISBN: 978-1-7328750-1-2

10 9 8 7 6 5 3 4 2 1

Editor: Liza Potter
Cover and Formatting: Streetlight Graphics

CHAPTER 1

VISIT TO THE WAY STATION

"There's a tree in the road, Pa," said Audrey, looking out the window of the stage.

"There was a rain storm last night," commented Brad. "The wind probably blew it down."

The driver slowed the stage and stopped it in front of the fallen tree. "Everybody out," hollered Jim Bates, the driver. "We've got to move that tree; there's no way I can drive this stage around it."

A masked man rose up behind a nearby bush, pointed his six-shooter at the driver and ordered, "Stay calm, no sudden moves, and no one gets hurt."

At that moment there was the crack of a rifle. The bullet hit a small boulder across the road, and the whine of the ricocheting bullet slowly faded away. "That was a reminder to keep everyone safe. One of my partners is at the top of the hill, so please do as I say."

"Do everything he asks," warned their father softly. "He just wants the money."

A horse whinnied in the distance as Jim Bates announced, "I'm reaching for the strongbox now; I'm not going for the shotgun."

"That's good;" said the masked man, "take it slow and easy."

Audrey heard the thud of the strongbox landing on the road and looked out the window and whispered, "Two more masked men are picking up the strongbox. The man with the pistol hasn't moved."

"They're taking it behind the trees," added Brad. "I don't see any horses; they're just standing with the box."

"Turn the stage around and go back to Riverton," commanded the man with the pistol.

Jim Bates gently flicked the reins and the horses started pulling as he released the brake. Turning to the right, the stage bumped over the rough ground, knocked down some small bushes and got back on the road.

"Just keep going and don't look back, or my friend with the rifle might get nervous and plug the curious one," laughed the masked man.

"Well, we won't visit the way station this morning," said their father, Harold Benton. He was the Riverton stage manager for Overland Stage, and his responsibilities included a monthly visit to the way station, several hours north of Riverton.

Harold Benton was a tall blue-eyed man with a small mustache. He had an inch-long scar on his right cheek from the battle at Gettysburg when he'd been a captain in the Union Army. After the war, he married Abigail, whom everyone called Abby. They moved to Riverton, where he began his job as the manager of the Riverton Overland Stage office.

"There's never been a holdup before, has there, Pa?"

questioned Brad. Brad was five foot four with dark wavy hair and blue eyes, just like his father.

Thirteen-year old Brad and his fourteen-year old sister, Audrey, were both in the seventh grade. Just after starting the first grade, she had taken ill with rheumatic fever and then the flu. Fortunately, she had fully recovered from both. However, the fever and the flu had caused her to miss most of the school year; so had started first grade again the following year, this time with her brother, Brad.

"Thankfully no one was hurt," said their father. "The Overland Stage Company discourages gunplay in a situation like this. We don't even have someone riding shotgun because we've never had a robbery in this area."

"Mr. Bates said they have guards when they move money or bullion to and from the gold and silver mines," said Brad.

"That's different," explained their father. "Gold and silver mines attract the criminal element, shysters, confidence men and the seamier side of society. Riverton is still small; it's a transportation hub with good farming and grazing. The highway men and undesirables aren't attracted to a stable community like Riverton.

It was noon when the stage rolled into Riverton. As was to be expected, the arrival of the stage attracted some attention. Since it was unscheduled, it attracted even more attention, and just about all the townspeople came out of the stores and shops.

Sheriff Tate looked to the drive expectantly and said, "Well?"

"We were robbed," replied Jim Bates, "this side of the way station. A tree blocked the road, I had to stop, and, well, they took the strongbox."

"Was anyone hurt?" queried Sheriff Tate.

"No, I followed the robber's orders, gave them the strongbox, and turned the stage around and returned to Riverton."

"I'll get a deputy, and we'll go to the holdup site. We may be able to follow their tracks," said the sheriff.

As Brad, Audrey and their father entered the stage office, their father said, "I've got to telegraph Overland's Denver office. They'll be working with the marshal in Denver about the robbery. Sheriff Tate and a deputy are going to the holdup site. They're looking for spent cartridges and other clues and evidence and should be back late this afternoon.

Audrey questioned, "How much was in the strongbox?"

"Twenty thousand dollars in gold and currency," replied her father. "I'll fill you in at supper. Until then, why don't you two go home and look at Brad's horse?"

Brad looked stunned; then, a big smile crept across his face as he asked, "Pa, my horse is at home?"

"Yes, Hank Lacy came into town today for some supplies, so he brought your horse with him. Now you two run along home, see Brad's horse, and help your grandmother with dinner."

For Brad's thirteenth birthday, his father had promised him a horse at the end of the school year. Tomorrow would be the last day of school, May 28, 1880.

Audrey had gotten Blaze when she turned thirteen.

Blaze was a small, black quarter horse with a white mark on her head.

As far as sisters go, Brad thought Audrey was all right. She was five foot two, slender, and had curly blond hair like her mother. She let Brad ride her horse, and they even rode double. They had planned to ride out to the Bar-X on Sunday to pick up Brad's horse.

And, as far as brothers go, Audrey thought Brad was all right, too. He almost always saddled her horse for her.

As Brad and Audrey started out the door, their father added, "The stage company requires that I write-up my own report of the robbery. I'll be visiting the site tomorrow afternoon. I thought you two might like to go with me. So, if you're interested, we'll leave right after lunch."

"Yes!" said Brad, "I want to go with you!"

"Me, too!" exclaimed Audrey.

"Then it's settled," said their father. "Tomorrow, right after lunch."

Brad and Audrey left the stage office and walked down the boardwalk past the general store and the bank.

"Gosh," said Audrey, "Pa sure is full of surprises. You get your horse today instead of Sunday. And, he's taking us to the holdup site tomorrow after lunch."

Brad kicked a small rock and said, "Sheriff Tate may have already looked for clues and evidence, but I want to look, too. How about you?"

Audrey grinned and said, "You know I do, or you wouldn't have even asked."

Walking a little faster, Brad said, "When a new horse is waiting for you, this walk home seems a lot longer."

"That's because we live in the country," Audrey replied. "A mile is 5,280 feet, but everyone knows a country mile is longer than a regular mile."

Brad wrinkled his forehead in thought and then said, "You're right, but I don't know how much longer. Maybe Pa can tell us how long a country mile is."

Brad didn't see Audrey purse her lips, but he heard her stifled laugh. He gave a playful jab at his sister and said, "Audrey, you suckered me again."

Audrey laughed and said, "Brad, a country mile is just an expression. But today, our walk home really does seem longer."

They were lucky to live only a mile from the school. Some of the students lived so far away, they had to ride their horses to school and keep them in the school stable during the day. In the winter, a few students even stayed with friends or relatives in Riverton during the week. They went home on weekends when the weather wasn't too bad.

The dust clung to their shoes as they walked down the road. Summer was near, and with it came the inevitable heat. It wasn't bad now, but in a month it would be much hotter. There was no breeze, and the late spring heat was broken only by the shade of scattered clumps of trees along the road. As they rounded the bend in the road, they could see their house, the barn, and the corral.

Audrey was jolted out of her silence when Brad shouted, "There she is! There's my horse!"

In the corral with Blaze was a black quarter horse with white markings on her front feet. Brad turned to his sister and asked, "Got any ideas for her name? I don't want to call her Blackie."

Audrey watched the new horse for a minute and said, "What about Coal, Midnight, Raven, Ebony, or Stormy?"

Brad replied, "I think I like Ebony, but I'm going to wait until tomorrow. We might think of a better name when we ride out to the robbery site."

"Let's see your horse before we go into the house," said his sister.

Brad walked up and gently stroked the horse's neck. "Nice girl. I see you're friends with Blaze. I'll bring you a carrot later."

The white markings on her front feet contrasted nicely with her shiny black coat. She was a pretty horse. Audrey watched Brad admire and make friends with his horse for a few minutes before saying, "We'd better wash up and start our chores."

"You're right," said Brad. "I'll have to wait until tomorrow to ride my horse."

Brad had finished his chores and was looking out the kitchen window as he washed up. There was a lot he wanted to know about his horse. *Is she fast? Is she smart? Can I teach her tricks?*

Audrey interrupted his thoughts: "Brad, I've already told Nana about the holdup. Your horse will still be there after dinner; come help us. Ma and Pa will be home any minute."

Brad dried his hands and face and took one last look at his horse. Then he turned around and watched his grandmother cooking dinner. "Hi Nana, how can I help?"

"You can start by setting the table," she said, putting her hand on his shoulder. "I see your Ma and Pa coming down the road now, so you better hurry."

Nana was Abby's mother, and their grandmother. Victoria Hanson was her formal name, but Brad and Audrey called her Nana. Nana's husband had been killed in the war. When Abby and Harold Benton had built their house in Riverton, they had asked her to come live with them. Victoria had accepted and left New York for Riverton fourteen years ago.

Brad set out five plates, knives, forks, and spoons. As he was getting the water glasses, Audrey brought in a bowl of boiled potatoes and said, "Ebony's a real nice looking horse. I can hardly wait to go riding with you tomorrow."

"You like the name Ebony too?" asked Brad. A big smile covered his face as he continued, "I thought that was the best name, but I didn't know you thought so too."

Harold and Abby Benton briefly stopped under the oak tree in the front yard and talked. A minute later, the young Bentons heard their parents walk across the front porch and open the front door.

"Victoria, dinner smells great," said Harold Benton as they entered the house.

Abby placed a stack of papers on the small table by the fireplace. Brad looked at her expectantly as she came toward the dining room. "Brad, with the excitement about the robbery, I didn't get much work done after school, so I had to bring some home."

Then, in a very serious voice, she continued, "Are we having a guest for dinner? I see a strange black horse in the corral."

"Ma!" exclaimed Brad, "That's my horse. Didn't Pa tell you?"

Her face blossomed with a big smile as she gave him a hug and replied, "I just wanted to be sure that you knew."

"Hank Lacy told me you've got a good horse," said his father. "She's comfortable with a saddle, and a number of the Bar-X men have ridden her. He also said they've treated her gently and that she's a very friendly horse. Did she take to you when you came home?"

"Yes," replied Brad. "She let me stroke her neck, and Blaze likes her."

"That's enough horse talk for now," said their grandmother. "The horse has already had her dinner, and ours is just about ready."

"I'm famished, and so is Abby. We'll wash-up and be right back," said their father as they went upstairs to wash off the day's dirt. Audrey straightened the napkins before joining Brad and Nana in the kitchen to make the final preparations for dinner.

A few minutes later their parents came down the stairs. Harold Benton stopped at the kitchen door and said, "That roast sure looks nice, Victoria."

"That was certainly a quick wash-up," replied Victoria. "You and Abby get yourselves seated while Audrey helps me finish the gravy. Then I want to hear about the holdup."

Nana brought in the roast while Audrey brought in the gravy. As soon as they were seated, their father said grace and began slicing the roast. Audrey held the plates and passed each one to the others in turn as her father carefully placed a slice of roast beef on each one. Lastly, he placed a slice on his own plate.

"I told Abby a little bit about the holdup on the way home," said their father. Looking at Victoria, he continued, "I haven't had time to tell you anything about it. I'll start at the beginning and tell you what Sheriff Tate discovered, and what he didn't discover, at the holdup site this afternoon."

He repeated what he had told Brad and Audrey that afternoon. Nana and Abby listened intently as he told about the tree across the road and the rifle shot.

Harold Benton continued, "Sheriff Tate found where the outlaws hid during the holdup. Some tree branches had been added to the bushes that the robbers had hidden behind. Those branches came from the tree that blocked the road, and that tree had been cut with a two-man saw. Sheriff Tate worked as a lumberjack years ago, so he could tell that the men who cut the tree were experienced lumberjacks."

"More coffee?" asked Audrey. Her father nodded and she filled his cup. Nana and Abby shook their heads to decline her offer.

"The robbers' horses had been tethered in a small stand of trees at the top of the ridge. Sheriff Tate followed their trail for about a half-mile before he lost it in the rocks. Tate's a good tracker, but he couldn't find the trail again. Maybe a first-rate mountain man could pick up the trail, but the sheriff couldn't. He didn't find any spent cartridges, food wrappings, liquor bottles, or footprints either. He said that other than where they tethered their horses and the professional tree cutting, he couldn't find any clues."

Looking directly at Brad and then Audrey, their father said, "I warned the sheriff that my two Pinkertons were going with me to the site tomorrow. He said that was fine, but that if we find any clues, we should bring them to him. He also warned me about trying to capture the robbers. The men are armed and would probably kill anyone who tried to capture them."

"I wouldn't want to try to capture armed men," agreed Audrey.

"I'm a good marksman with Pa's rifle," said Brad. "I'm pretty good on a horse too, but I don't want to tangle with the robbers."

"Right," said Audrey, "but I would like to practice the tracking techniques that Running Bear taught us last year."

"Tracking is what needs to be done," said their father. "If we can find a few more clues at the site, maybe Sheriff Tate will be able to find the robbers. And," he said, pausing dramatically as he looked at Brad and then slowly turned his head toward Audrey, "we just might be able to pick up their trail."

Audrey was clearing the table when Nana brought in an apple pie from the kitchen. "I know you've all saved room for some apple pie," she said, setting it on the table.

"I always have room for your apple pie. Did you add some blackberries?" asked Harold Benton.

"Of course she did," said Audrey. "We canned fifty pints last summer." Then a worried look appeared on her face and she continued, "They are in the pie, aren't they, Nana?"

Nana smiled and said, "Have I ever made an apple pie without adding blackberries? Why, blackberries add a lively taste to an otherwise bland apple pie."

Their father finished his coffee and pushed his chair back from the table. Then, crossing his right leg over his left knee, he said, "Abby, how'd your day go?"

She told about the last full day at school, and, of course, Sheriff Tate's announcement of the stage holdup and what the other teachers had said about it. Nana told them about her day, as did Brad and Audrey.

Abby Benton looked at Brad and Audrey and said, "While you three are doing your detective work tomorrow, I'll be practicing a new hymn for Sunday: "God of Our Fathers." Nana's friend in Vermont sent me a copy. Reverend Daniel Roberts wrote the text and set it to the music of "Russian Hymn" for the 1876 Fourth of July centennial celebration.

Their mother added, "Reverend Roberts is the rector of St. Thomas' Church in Brandon, Vermont. Their choir performed it for the first time at their Fourth of July service in 1876. It's a great hymn. Reverend Roberts has sent it to the Episcopal Church's commission that is revising their hymnal."

"The commission that's revising the Episcopal hymnal?" questioned Victoria Hanson.

"Yes," said Abby. "The words for the first verse are:

> God of our fathers, whose almighty hand
> Leads forth in beauty all the starry band
> Of shining worlds in splendor thro' the skies

Our grateful songs before Thy throne arise.

I've been hoping to find a new hymn that can become as popular as "Old Hundred," and I think this can be that hymn."

"What's Old Hundred," asked Brad.

"The first phrase is: "Praise God, from whom all blessings flow," said their mother.

"We do sing that one a lot," said Brad. "I like it, but it would be nice to have another good hymn."

"That's why I'm practicing "God of Our Fathers," she said. "So, the three of you better not get caught by those robbers."

"Ma," huffed Brad, "we won't get caught. We're just going to look for clues and try to find their tracks. We'll give the clues to Sheriff Tate and show him where we found their tracks."

"Abby," said Harold Benton, "we don't want to meet up with the robbers. We want to be in Riverton when Congressman Garfield comes through next week."

"Congressman Garfield!" she exclaimed. "Why, he might be picked as a candidate for President when the Republicans meet in Chicago next week. I know he's not the most likely one, but I've got a hunch he's going to end up the nominee."

Nana smiled, cocked her head to one side, and closed one eye as she looked at her son-in-law and sternly said, "Harold P. Benton, have you been holding out on me?"

"Victoria," he laughed, "I know better than to try to keep something from you. I just got the news this afternoon. The telegraph operator at the train station brought me the message. I don't have the exact date, but Congressman James A. Garfield will be passing through Riverton on a special train."

"The train has to stop for water," said their mother. "I expect he'll probably greet the mayor and give a speech."

"I'm sure he'll give a speech," added their father. "He's been in Congress since 1863. He's been the leader of the House Republicans since '76 and just got elected to the Senate this January. And...," he said with a dramatic pause, "this is an election year. He'll probably spend an hour or so in Riverton before going on."

"The last election train I saw had a detachment of soldiers on it," said Victoria. "Did the message say whether soldiers would be on the train?"

"There was no mention of soldiers in the telegram. I don't think there'll be soldiers on the train because he's not the president. However, I'm sure he's hired the Pinkerton Detective Agency to protect him, so there will probably be some Pinkertons on the train."

The family talked about the coming election for another hour. Nana told stories about past presidents and past elections. She talked about the events that led to the election of Abraham Lincoln and those that led to the Civil War.

"Nana, you mean two main causes of the Civil War were states' rights and slavery?" asked Audrey.

Nana smiled and replied, "Yes, those were two of the causes. It was a clash of two different cultures, the industrial North versus the agricultural South. The southern states felt more rights should rest with the state governments than the federal government. They felt that free trade and a federation of strong state governments was best for their agricultural economy."

"Tobacco, sugarcane, and cotton are their primary exports," said their father. "The operation of a plantation requires many people, whether hired hands or slaves."

Their grandmother continued, "The northern states wanted a powerful federal government and weak state governments. This would help standardize trade policies and impose tariffs on selected imported goods to protect northern industries. This would be better for their industrialized economy. The South, however, wanted to buy lower priced manufactured goods from other countries. It was a clash of the North's industrial culture with the South's agricultural culture."

"The slavery issue was also a tremendous factor," said Abby Benton. "The antislavery agitation in the North worried the South. If slavery were abolished, it would change the economy in the South. Slaves were property that worked without pay and could be bought and sold. If slavery were abolished, fortunes would be destroyed."

"But slavery is wrong," interjected Brad.

"So is taking something and not paying for it," explained Nana. "Some southerners viewed abolishing ownership of slaves the same way Hank Lacy would view abolishing ownership of cattle. It's not right to take a man's property without paying him."

"It was not a simple issue," said their mother. "That's why the South decided to secede and establish the Confederate States of America. Their new government was supportive of their agricultural economy."

"President Lincoln said no, they couldn't secede.

The result was the Civil War," explained their father. "It was a war that killed or wounded over a million men. Twenty percent of all Union soldiers were killed; twenty-five percent of all Confederate soldiers were killed. The war destroyed farms, plantations, bridges, railroads, and cities. Crops were destroyed and farm animals killed. People died from illness and disease caused by the hardships of war."

Brad and Audrey continued to ask questions, and their parents and grandmother seemed to have all the answers. Their parents told about life in the United States at the time Lincoln was elected. Harold recalled that while he was serving as a Captain in the Union Army, Garfield had served as a Colonel and was eventually appointed Major General—-for gallantry at Chickamauga.

"What does he look like?" asked Brad.

"He's a big man, six feet tall, weighs about two hundred pounds," replied his father. "He is also an ordained minister."

"An ordained minister?" questioned Abby.

"That's right. Reverend Garfield, Disciple of Christ. He preaches a powerful sermon and really has a way with men."

"What a history lesson," said Audrey.

"Yes, and much more interesting than history at school," added Brad.

"I don't like to interrupt scholarly research," said their mother, "but it's getting late. Besides, I know two young Pinkertons who need to finish their chores and get to bed."

Abby Benton picked up her stack of school papers,

sat down at the end of the oak dining table, and began writing. Her husband had started building the table just after they got married. Many evenings had been spent sanding the boards he'd gotten from the sawmill to get a tight fit and a smooth top. Abby's friends admired the beautiful table, and she enjoyed telling them that it was Harold's present to her for their first wedding anniversary. Because he couldn't work on the table full time, it had taken him six months from the day he started until it was complete. Most of the work was done in the winter.

Nana helped Brad clear the table as Audrey brought the dishpan from the back porch. She scraped a bar of soap several times with a knife, flaking the soap into the dishpan. Taking the kettle off the kitchen woodstove, she poured some hot water into the dishpan and the rest into the stoppered kitchen sink. Next, she pumped some cold water from the well into the sink and dishpan until the water in both was a comfortable temperature.

Brad and Audrey had worked out a regular method for washing the dishes. Audrey washed them in the dishpan, rinsed them in the sink, and then handed them to Brad to dry. While doing the dishes, Brad and Audrey talked about the robbery and discussed how to find and follow someone's tracks.

"Brad, do you think we might find some clues the sheriff didn't find?" asked Audrey as she handed him the last plate to dry.

Brad put the plate in the cabinet and hung the towel on a peg to dry and replied, "Yes, Running Bear taught us a lot about tracking. He said it's important to think like the person you're tracking. When we get to the holdup site tomorrow, we have to look for the smallest details. I don't think we'll find a hat with the robber's name in it, but we may find a boot print that can help us learn more about the robbers."

Audrey gave Brad a quizzical look and asked, "How can a boot print tell us about the robbers?"

"Remember Miss Butler, our fourth grade teacher? She couldn't find her spectacles because she had pushed them up on top of her head. She looked on her desk and in her purse and still couldn't find them. That's what most people do with a clue. They have the clue, just like Miss Butler had her glasses. But just like she didn't see her glasses, many people can't see the clues. If we study the clues the way Running Bear would, we may learn something about the robbers."

"We've finished the dishes," said Audrey. "I'm going to say good night to Ma, Pa, and Nana and then go to bed."

Their father looked up as Brad and Audrey came into the living room. Before they could say anything, he said, "I see two very tired young Bentons. It's important that you get a good night's rest because tomorrow's going to be a long, hard day. Finish your chores and hit the sack."

One of Brad's chores was to keep the kitchen woodbox full. The woodbox would hold about two days' supply of wood for the kitchen stove. If Nana did a lot of baking, however, he'd have to refill it after one day. More wood was stored in a small shed behind the house.

Each summer, Brad and his father would take the wagon, a two-man saw, and a couple of axes to the mountains and bring back wood for the year. It took them several days to cut a year's supply. Once the wood was cut, the larger pieces had to be split. This was done in the fall after the wood had dried. Wood also had to be split into kindling, the very small pieces necessary to start a fire. Brad usually split the kindling every few weeks and put it in the kindling box in the woodshed.

As Brad went to the shed, he saw Ebony and Blaze in the corral. "Ebony, I'll get you a carrot from the root cellar after I take in the wood. I'll get one for you too, Blaze." Blaze nickered.

Brad loaded his arms with wood and returned to the kitchen. He made two more trips to heap the box with wood. Then he went to the root cellar, brushed back the dirt and straw, and picked out two large carrots.

"Got a treat for the horses?" asked Audrey as Brad headed to the corral.

"Some carrots," he replied. "I want Ebony to feel at home. And I can't ignore Blaze, so I have a carrot for her too. Come on."

"That's why I'm here. I'll feed Blaze while you get to know Ebony."

"I told them I'd bring them a carrot after I finished filling the woodbox. Blaze nickered after I said that. Do you think she understood?"

"I don't know. I think animals understand more than most people think they do. Blaze probably recognized her name when you spoke to her. Besides, we often give her a carrot before we go to bed, so she's probably expecting one."

"Well, here's a carrot for Blaze. I'll give this one to Ebony."

"Come on, girl," coaxed Brad, "I've got a carrot for you."

Ebony took the carrot from Brad and munched it down. Brad looked at the small mountains north of the corral. The large mountains farther north were still snowcapped.

"Tomorrow we'll be riding into the mountains," said Brad. "I hope we find some clues."

"We will. Running Bear taught us a lot last summer. We'll find some clues, but it won't be easy to find new ones. Sheriff Tate is a good tracker."

"Tomorrow will be a full day," commented Brad. "We finish school in the morning and come home for lunch. Then, we go to the holdup site with Pa."

Brad and Audrey left the corral and walked back to the house. It was a nice house; it was two stories, with five bedrooms upstairs and a root cellar under the kitchen. A large, covered porch faced the road. It was one of the larger houses in Riverton.

"I thought I'd find you two at the corral," said their father. "You'll be able to ride your new horse tomorrow, Brad. It's going to be a long day, so you need to be rested. Your grandmother is already in bed."

As Brad and Audrey went up the stairs to their bedrooms, their father added, "I know you two will find some clues tomorrow. Bear's a good teacher."

CHAPTER 2
THE SEARCH FOR CLUES

Nana walked down the hallway and knocked on Audrey's door. "Time to get up, Miss Pinkerton."

Audrey sat up on the edge of her bed and thought, Miss Pinkerton? Then she remembered that she was going to the holdup site with Brad and her father. She dressed quickly and was washing her face when there was another knock on her door.

"Hurry up, Audrey," said Brad. "Breakfast is ready. Ebony and Blaze have had their apples, and we can't be late for school."

Audrey looked in the mirror at her wet face in disbelief. She asked herself, *what happened? Brad got up before I did? Ebony? Oh, his new horse. He's already been out to see his horse!*

Audrey dried her wet face and then combed her blond hair. She quickly straightened her bed, looked in the mirror approvingly, and then headed for the dining room. Nana, Ma and Pa, and Brad were already seated. Being the last one at the breakfast table was rare for Audrey, who was usually one of the first. Her mother looked up, saw Audrey's worried expression, and said; "You're not late, dear, Nana just got up a little earlier than usual."

"I woke up early so I could check on Ebony," said Brad. "I got a couple of apples from the cellar on my way to the corral. Ebony was at the fence waiting for me. She ate the apple out of my hand."

"You've got a good horse, Brad," said his father. "Take care of her, and she'll take care of you."

"The horses are fine, but breakfast is getting cold," said Victoria. She looked at her son-in law and said, "Harold?"

Harold Benton said a short prayer and everyone started breakfast. Audrey poured coffee for her parents and Nana. Her father helped himself to some fried potatoes and then passed the plate on. Abby did the same with the ham and eggs, while Nana started the biscuit plate. Brad and his father wolfed down their breakfast while Abby, Audrey and Nana ate more slowly. No one talked for a few minutes.

Nana always ate sparingly at breakfast, so she finished first. She pushed her chair about two feet away from the table. Then she looked at Harold and said, "I want to make sure I've planned the meals right for today. I'll have lunch ready for you and your two Pinkertons at noon. Detectives work best with full stomachs." Turning toward her daughter, she continued, "Abby, you said the children get out at eleven o'clock, but the teachers work a full day. So, I've packed you a lunch; it's on top of your school papers. For dinner, I expect everyone will be home by five-thirty, as usual."

Nana was silent for a moment, and then continued, "We'll probably have venison for dinner. I promised an apple pie to Len Reno the next time he brought me some venison. Yesterday he stopped by and told me was going hunting first thing this morning."

"If Len's going deer hunting this morning, we'll have venison tonight," chuckled Harold Benton. "I've never known him to get skunked. You'd better make that pie."

Abby Benton finished her coffee and stood up. "Audrey, Brad, let's get going. You don't want to be late the last day of school."

"I'd better get a move-on too," said their father. I've got to talk to Sheriff Tate about Congressman Garfield's visit next week."

Abby Benton entered the school, while Brad and Audrey stayed outside to tell their friends what they knew about the robbery. Buck Hodges and Harry Acker hung on every word as Brad described the robbery. Wilma Sue Bevins looked at Audrey several times in disbelief. Audrey nodded in agreement to what Brad was telling them.

"Audrey, did the robbers really fire a rifle over the stage?" asked Wilma Sue.

"Yes, just like Brad said. We heard the shot and the whine of the ricocheting bullet."

"That was a smart move by the robbers," said Buck. "The passengers and driver couldn't see him, and that meant no gun play."

Harry was quiet as he thought about what Brad had said. Harry-the-Thinker, as his friends sometimes called him, was very good at looking at a difficult problem and seeing a simple solution. Harry was, in many ways, like Running Bear. He could solve tough problems the way Running Bear could track tough trails. Harry-the-Thinker saw things most people couldn't readily see.

Looking at Brad and Buck, Harry said, "The robbers knew the stage was carrying the money. One of them probably knows somebody at the Riverton bank or somebody at the bank in Denver. The stage always carries a strongbox, even if it's empty, right?"

"That's the rule," said Brad. "That way, only the bank knows when there's money in it. Even Overland doesn't know whether the box has money, newspapers, rocks, or gold."   Abby Benton stepped out of the front door and rang the large bell with her hand to start the last day of school. Brad and Audrey hurried off to class with their friends.

Brad thought, *only a few more hours until school is out, then we can go to the holdup site.*

Audrey poked him in the ribs as they entered the room. "Wake up, Brad. Stop thinking about the holdup and Ebony for a few more hours. You'll get to ride her when we go to the holdup site after lunch."

"You're right, but it's hard to think about school when I think about this afternoon."

"Hello, Audrey," said Miss Jones as Audrey entered the room. "I want to thank you for your help by tutoring some of the students this year. It has meant a lot to me and to them."

"Thanks, Miss Jones. When you said I'd learn more by helping others, I didn't believe you. But now that I've done it a year, I know what you mean. I did learn a lot just by helping my friends."

When all the students had arrived, Miss Jones had them empty their desks and put their books on the shelves in the closet. Next, the students washed the blackboard, the desks, and the large table.

She announced that everyone was promoted to the next grade.

Some students, however, would have to review their arithmetic during the summer because they had done poorly. Without the review, Miss Jones said they would have a very difficult time in the eighth grade. Betty Jones and Angus McTavish had already asked for help. Harry Acker said he'd help Angus, since he lived close to the McTavish farm. Wilma Sue was going to help Betty because they lived close to each other. Brad and Audrey, Harry and Angus, and Betty and Wilma Sue had agreed to meet after church each Sunday and review their arithmetic lessons.

The seventh-graders all wanted to stay in class together, especially since Riverton was starting a high school in a year. Most towns provided public school only through the sixth or eighth grade. Riverton was going to make it possible for the students to continue going to school locally through high school.

"Class, it's just about time for dismissal," said Miss Jones. "I'm going to Denver later this summer to see my parents. I'll be back in September, and I want to see all of you here." She always said something personal to each student at the end of the year. Brad wondered what she was going to say to him.

"Brad, take care of your new horse. Audrey, you be careful when you go to the holdup site this afternoon. Harry, read something other than Shakespeare. Your father's hotel has many good books in its library. He's well educated and loves to read. Try Aristotle, Caesar, and some of the other great books."

Abby Benton stepped into the hall and rang the

bell, ending the school day. The clanging of the large hand-held bell reverberated through the building as the students headed for the doors.

"Goodbye, Miss Jones," said Audrey. "Have a good trip."

"I will have a good trip because I know that you'll be helping Angus and Betty. They're good people, the kind that Riverton needs. The Sunday reviews will really help. Have a good summer."

Brad and Audrey and the other students ran homeward full tilt, eager to start their long-awaited vacation activities. After running halfway home, Audrey gasped, "Brad, let's walk. We've run over half a mile."

Also panting, Brad slowed to a walk. Audrey grabbed his shoulder for support as she walked beside him. Breathing heavily, she asked, "Do you think we'll beat Pa home?"

Looking at his sister, he replied, "Of course. Something always happens at the last minute to make Pa late. What makes you think today will be different?"

The house was shaded from the summer sun by two large oak trees in the front yard. A row of junipers on the north side of the house provided a windbreak from the cold winter winds. As Audrey and Brad rounded the bend in the road, they saw Ebony and Blaze standing in the shade of the oaks.

"I see smoke from the kitchen chimney," said Brad. "Maybe Nana made two pies, one for Mr. Reno and one for us."

Audrey grabbed Brad's arm and began walking a little faster. "We still have enough of the blackberries we canned for twenty pies. And Nana always makes two or more pies at the same time."

Brad and Audrey got home a little before noon. The smell of apple-blackberry pie filled the house.

"We're home, Nana," said Brad and Audrey in unison as they entered the front door.

"Venison for supper?" asked Brad

"Of course, Len Reno brought over the ribs and a roast this morning. He put the rest of the deer in his icehouse."

Brad knew about the icehouse. Several years earlier, Len Reno had built the large log building into the side of a hill. The log walls were covered on the outside with earth. Inside, there was an additional wall of boards with sawdust sandwiched between it and the logs. The floor was made of rocks covered with boards. If the door were opened only early in the morning, the ice would last through the summer and into the winter. The Riverton Hotel used several blocks of ice a day. In addition, Harry Reno's icehouse stored meat for the Hotel and Hans Finster, the butcher.

Brad and his father had helped Mr. Reno cut blocks of ice for the icehouse that spring. They'd worked all day cutting ice and loading it into the wagon. Angus McTavish had provided the team of draft horses and heavy wagon to haul the ice.

"Wash up, have a seat, and let's eat," said their father.

"You're home!" said Brad. "I thought you'd be late."

"No, I've been home for about half an hour. Wanted to make sure the venison stew was on schedule for tonight."

"Chili and corn bread for lunch," announced Nana

as she brought a large bowl of chili to the table. "The corn bread will be ready by the time you Pinkertons have washed up."

Brad and Audrey went to the kitchen pump and quickly washed the dust from their face and hands. Brad picked up the plate of hot corn bread and followed Nana to the table while Audrey pumped a pitcher of cool well water.

Their father said grace. Then, for a few minutes, everyone ate in silence. The sound of soupspoons and the gentle clinking of water glasses broke the stillness of the noon meal.

Brad was the first to speak. "Pa, do you have any more information about the robbery?"

"Nothing since yesterday, but I think we'll find some clues this afternoon that will help Sheriff Tate capture the robbers."

Nana looked at the empty bowls and said, "If you find new clues as fast as you ate that chili, the case will be closed before church on Sunday."

"I hope you're right," said their father. "We'd best saddle up and move out." He pushed his chair back and stood up. "It'll take us a little under an hour to get there. I've got a canteen of water for each of us. Tie it to your saddle and snug it down."

Harold Benton strapped on his pistol, put on his hat, picked up his rifle, and opened the back door.

"See you tonight, Nana," said Audrey, as she gave Nana a quick hug.

Nana followed them to the door. "The stew and pie will be waiting," she said as they went to the corral.

Brad saddled Ebony under the watchful eye of his

father. While their father saddled his own horse, Brad and Audrey led theirs out of the corral and tied them to the hitching rail. Brad tied the canteen to his saddle and snugged it down. Audrey did the same with hers. By the time they'd finished, their father had saddled his horse and left the corral.

"Looks like my Pinkertons are ready. Mount up, and we'll get going." Their father squeezed the flanks of his horse and started off at a fast trot. Audrey and Brad did the same and quickly fell in on each side of their father.

"Pa, I was hoping you had heard something new about the robbery," said Brad.

"Nothing today, the latest is what I told you last night."

This was the first time the three of them had ridden together. Their father sat straight in the saddle, just as he had 15 years earlier as a captain in the Union Army. Audrey, on his right, also rode well, sitting straight and gently holding the reins in her left hand. Brad on his left, also sat straight in the saddle, holding the reins firmly, but gently. Each one rode as an extension of the horse, not just as a rider sitting in a saddle on top of the horse.

They rode in relative silence to the holdup site. To Brad, enjoying his first ride on Ebony, it seemed only a few minutes later that his father motioned down the road.

"The holdup site is just around the next bend." He pointed to the steep hill on the left. "They did a clever job planning the holdup. There are lots of boulders, trees, and bushes to hide behind. They also had an excellent view of the road. The stage wouldn't have had a chance even if it'd had an armed escort."

"There's the tree that blocked the road," said Audrey.

"And there's the stump," said Brad.

Harold Benton stopped, dismounted, and looped his reins across a large branch. "Tie your horses up and join me in the center of the road. We'll talk through the holdup. We want to be very careful when we start looking for clues. We want to find clues, not destroy them."

Audrey and Brad did as their father had instructed and joined him in the middle of the road.

"The stage stopped opposite this large boulder, which would be about here." Their father nodded to the boulder. Then he motioned down the road and continued. "Three armed men wearing masks came out of hiding as soon as the stage stopped -— one in front of the stage and two behind it."

"Probably those bushes by those big trees," said Brad, pointing to a few large oak trees. "The other trees are too small to hide behind."

"And there's the bushes with tree branches that Sheriff Tate told you about," said Audrey pointing to the bushes.

Looking at the crest of the steep hill, their father continued. "That's probably the rock the sharpshooter was behind during the holdup. The late morning sun would be behind his back, making it almost impossible for anyone on the road to see him."

Brad and Audrey shaded their eyes and looked at the crest of the hill. It was early afternoon, but the overhead sun still made it hard to see what was on the crest.

"Well, let's get started," said their father. "We'll start with that tree stump. Walk slowly, and look before you step. We don't want to destroy any clues."

The three of them left the road and slowly walked abreast of each other to the tree stump. Brad approached from the left, Audrey from the right, and their father in the center. They examined the ground before each step.

"Pa! I found a bolt!" exclaimed Audrey as she held it up for him to see.

Harold Benton looked at it and said, "Good. I'll put it in this sack. Now look for the nut that goes with it. The bolt could be from the saw."

When they finally reached the tree stump, Harold said, "Now, let's take a step to the left and then go back to the road. We may see something we missed."

No new clues were found on the way back to the road. "Gosh, Pa, we didn't find anything," said Brad. He stuck his hands in his pockets, shrugged his shoulders and kicked a small rock.

"We may not find anything else. But we won't know that until we've looked. Let's look at the opposite side of the road, the side the robbers weren't on." Their father gave a beckoning wave to Brad and Audrey. When they were together again, he continued, "We'll walk along the road side by side. Do it the same way we did it before. Walk slowly, and look ahead and to each side before taking a step."

When they were about fifty yards from the holdup site, their father announced, "Okay, let's turn around and go back. Audrey, stay where you are, Brad and I'll go to the downhill side for the return."

The dullness of the return was broken when Brad stopped and picked up a half-used plug of chewing tobacco. "Ugh! I don't know why people chew this stuff. It smells awful and turns your mouth brown. Is this a clue, Pa?"

"It could be, put it in the sack with the bolt. Sheriff Tate will decide if it's useful. Now, let's check out the bushes where the robbers hid."

Abreast on the side of the road again, their father continued. "Okay, let's head for the bushes on the right. We'll do it the same way we've been doing it."

The Bentons searched for clues as they went to the first group of bushes, but found nothing. They continued to search as they returned to the road, but again, nothing was found. They repeated the process for the second and third clumps of bushes. Again, no clues were found.

"Is this what detective work is all about?" asked Brad as he wiped the sweat from his forehead. "We've been out here half an hour and all we've found is a bolt and half a plug of chewing tobacco."

Their father walked to his horse and took out his canteen. After taking a long drink, he poured some water on his kerchief. As he wiped his forehead and neck, he replied. "Yes, detective work is a lot of work for a few clues. Sometimes there aren't any clues. I hope the two clues we found will help Sheriff Tate."

Brad and Audrey took a drink from their canteens, moistened their kerchiefs, and wiped their face and necks as their father had done. Audrey looked at the crest of the hill and said, "We've still got the sharpshooter's boulder to search."

"That's right. I take it you're ready to make the climb." Their father picked up a straight branch to use as a walking stick and started toward the boulder at the crest of the hill.

"We're with you, Pa," said Audrey, as she put her hand on Brad's shoulder. "Shouldn't we search for clues on the way up?"

Their father started up the hill. He answered Audrey's question as they slowly climbed toward the crest. "When you're a detective, you always look for clues. You even look for clues when you're going someplace to look for clues. That's why Pinkertons are so good. They're always doing their job."

At the crest of the hill, they breathed heavily as they turned around and looked down at the road. Harold took his wet kerchief and wiped his face and neck. "Not much shade up here, except at that boulder."

"Should we search side by side again?" asked Brad.

"Right, three abreast again, maybe we'll find something."

The three started their search as they moved slowly toward the sharpshooter's boulder. As they reached the boulder, Audrey said, "Nothing, not one single clue."

"Don't get discouraged," said Brad. "We found two clues the sheriff missed. And we still have the rest of the boulder area to search."

"You're right. The sheriff would have found the clues

if they were obvious. This is a very rocky area, not a meadow, so there are not any boot prints."

"And the robbers probably took the obvious clues with them," said Brad. "Clues like hats with their name written inside and spent cartridges."

"We'll start the search on the other side of the boulder. We're almost done," said their father.
They lined up again and slowly started their search on the other side of the boulder. About 50 feet past the boulder, they turned and started back to the boulder on the downside of the hill.

As they got closer to the boulder, Brad saw a flash in the bushes. "Wait, I saw something. I'm going to back up." Backing up, he again saw something gleam in the clump of grass. He slowly walked to it, picked up an odd-shaped piece of metal and gave it to his father.

"That looks like a metal toecap for a boot, Brad. You may have found a good clue," said his father, dropping the piece of metal in the sack. "Let's keep looking."

A search of the entire area around the boulder brought no additional clues. Heads and necks were again wiped with kerchiefs before their father announced, "We'd best be heading back. I'll get these clues over to Sheriff Tate. This bolt, the half-used plug of chewing tobacco, and the metal toecap for a boot are interesting clues that may help him come up with something."

They carefully zigzagged down the side of the mountain to the road. Once again on the road, they took their canteens from their saddles and drank. Then they mounted up and started home at a trot. Halfway home, they stopped at a small stream to rest and let their horses drink some water.

Brad looked at his father and asked, "You'll be home around five-thirty as usual, won't you?"

"I expect so. I'll give these clues to Sheriff Tate, write my report, and come home. If the sheriff has any more news, I'll tell you about it at dinner. Let's mount up and get going."

The three swung into their saddles and started back home. A little later they reached the rutted road to their house. Brad and Audrey turned off the road to Riverton and headed home. Their father continued on to Riverton.

"We'd better wipe down the horses and give them some oats after that ride," said Audrey.

"Right, I'll take off the saddles and put them in the tack room while you get the oats. We can wipe them down while they're eating."

Audrey brought out two feed bags with oats and a couple of horse towels. They wiped the horses in silence. Afterwards, they removed the feed bags and put them back in the tack room.

"How about a pump bath" asked Audrey? "I'm dusty and sticky and I'm sure you are too. I'll get thc towels."

Brad smiled, "It's a deal. The only thing better would be a swim in the creek, but we don't have time for that."

Audrey ran to the house to get a couple of towels while Brad went to the horse trough and started pumping. The water had filled the trough and was overflowing by the time she returned.

"You're first, Audrey. I'm second." As Brad pumped,

Audrey stuck her head under the spout and let the water clean her head and neck. Audrey dried her head and hands, and then she switched places with Brad.

"This is cold!" exclaimed Brad when his sister finished pumping several times. "Why didn't you tell me it was so cold?"

"It's always this cold. It just feels colder because you're so hot. And, cool or cold, we'd better hurry up so we can help Nana with dinner."

"Right," said Brad. "Ma and Pa will be home shortly."

"Maybe he'll have heard something from the bank in Denver," said Audrey.

CHAPTER 3
TRACKING THE ROBBERS

"Victoria, that venison stew was great," said Harold Benton wiping his mouth with his napkin.

Nana smiled and said, "Mr. Reno has his apple pie. I'll be making him another pie for tomorrow. He'll be stopping by with a roast late tomorrow afternoon. We'll have that for Sunday dinner."

Brad and Audrey cleared the dishes off the table. Audrey brought in a pot of coffee and refilled her father's cup.

Brad brought in the pie, five plates, and a butcher knife. As Brad was cutting the pie, his father described their afternoon search for clues. Audrey had served the last piece of pie when Brad asked, "What did Sheriff Tate say about the clues?"

"The sheriff said that the metal toecap may be important. He showed it to Christopher Schmitt, the boot maker. Schmitt said if someone comes in to have a metal toecap replaced, he'll let the sheriff know." Harold Benton took another bite of apple pie and looked at Brad and Audrey. "The bolt won't help unless we find someone with a saw missing a bolt. And, unfortunately, the chewing tobacco probably won't help either. 'Old

Blue' is a common brand. It could have been dropped by anyone using the road."

"Did the sheriff have any other information about the holdup?" asked Audrey.

"Yes, and it looks like your schoolmate, Harry-The-Thinker, was right on target. The Overland office in Denver wired me that only two bank employees knew what was in the strongbox. And, it seems that one of them, Clete Collins, resigned Wednesday morning. The federal marshal in Denver is trying to find him now."

"Pa, we'd like to go back to the holdup site tomorrow. Is that okay?" asked Brad.

"As long as you get your chores done, you have my permission."

Harold Benton looked at his wife, her blond hair highlighted by the late afternoon sun coming through the window. "Is that okay with you, Abby?"

"I'm concerned that you two might meet up with the robbers. But it has been two days since the robbery, so they're sure to be far away by now. It should be all right. But I want you two to stick together. Don't do anything dangerous, and--," their mother paused and then continued, "You're both responsible and law abiding. I don't have to lecture you about what to do. You've been doing the right things for years and I'm proud of you." Then with a stern look she said, "Be back in time for dinner." Her face broadened into a smile and she added, "You hear?"

Brad had just gotten into bed when Audrey knocked on the door, "Brad, can we talk?"

"Sure, come on in." Brad sat up as his sister came in and sat on the edge of the bed.

"Brad, I'm excited about tomorrow, but I'm also scared. What if the robbers come back?"

Brad looked at his sister questioningly. "Why would the robbers come back? They've already got the money. That's the last place they'd want to be. They're on their way to wherever by now. Besides, if we see something suspicious, we can always come back home. We don't have to stay at the holdup site any longer than we want to."

Audrey wrinkled her forehead and looked at her brother. "You're right, that's the last place they'd want to be." She stood up and went to the door, turned around and said, "If you wake up before me, get me up. I'll do the same for you."

Brad grinned, "It's a deal. First one up gets the other one up. See you in the morning."

Brad woke up when he heard Nana go down the stairs. The sun was just rising as he got up and washed the night off his face. He got dressed, straightened his bed, and combed his hair. Then he went down the hall to Audrey's room and knocked on the door. "Audrey," he said softly, "time to get up. I'm going down to help Nana. Meet you in the kitchen."

Audrey threw off the covers and jumped out of bed. *Brad beat me getting up again. He woke up early so he could see his horse.* She quickly washed her face and got dressed.

"Good morning, Miss Pinkerton," said Nana. "Brad's out giving Ebony a carrot; said he'd be back in a minute."

Just then Brad opened the door. "I brought in some more wood." He put an armload of wood in the box behind the stove. "With what I brought in last night, this should keep you going through Sunday."

Nana looked at her two grandchildren. "I suppose you two would like to get going. How about some pancakes?"

"That'd be great," said Brad as he washed the dirt off his hands.

"I'll pack you a lunch too," said Nana. "I expect detectives get hungry, even Pinkertons."

After breakfast, Audrey cleared the table as Brad went to the cellar to get some apples. Nana opened the breadbox and pulled out a loaf. She cut four slices for the sandwiches as Audrey watched.

Audrey slowly shook her head in wonderment and said; "Nana, you slice the bread so," Audrey paused thoughtfully, and then continued, "so perfectly. I hope I can learn to slice bread like you."

"It takes time, and practice, but you can do it." Nana finished slicing the bread and set down the knife. Then she opened the icebox and got a chunk of venison. Her eyes twinkled as she continued, "I cooked some extra venison for sandwiches when I made the stew. Venison sandwiches ought to taste right nice about noon."

Brad returned from the cellar with four apples. After washing and drying them, he put them on the counter where Nana was packing the lunches.

Nana finished packing the lunches and handed a small cloth lunch bag to Audrey and another one to Brad. "I packed a lunch for each of you. A couple of apples, a venison sandwich, a hard-boiled egg, a piece of apple-blackberry pie, and some corn bread. That should last you till dinner tonight. Why, you'll even have enough to share with a robber."

Brad grinned, "We're not going to see any robbers. And if we do, they're not getting any of my lunch."

"Mine either," chirped Audrey as they went out the door. "Say goodbye to Ma and Pa for us. See you tonight!"

Audrey brought Blaze and Ebony into the barn and Brad placed the saddle on Blaze. Audrey was older, but Brad was stronger. It was easier for him than for her to put the saddle on the back of her horse. Once the saddle was on the horse, though, Audrey could finish the job. As Brad was saddling Ebony, he thought about what his father had told him a year before. "Brad, your sister may be older, but you're the man. You're stronger than she is. That's the way God made us. It has nothing to do with her illness as a child; she's fully recovered from that. A man's supposed to do the hard work a woman can't do. That goes for you and your sister. You do the things that require strength. She'll appreciate it and give to you in return."

Pa had been right. He'd saddled Blaze for Audrey last summer, and Audrey had always let him ride her horse.

"I'm ready," said Audrey as she mounted her horse. "I'll race you to the road."

"I'll be ready as soon as I finish tying my canteen down." Brad mounted Ebony and came aside his sister. Then he stopped and said, "On the count of three. One! Two! Three!"

Sensing the excitement, the horses broke into a fast gallop. Ebony slowly pulled ahead, and by the time they reached the road she was ahead by two lengths. Brad gently pulled back on the reins and Ebony slowed to a comfortable trot. Blaze came alongside and the two horses matched gaits.

"Wow!" said Brad. "Ebony's fast! I never thought she'd be able to beat Blaze, especially by two lengths."

Audrey smiled in amazement, "Neither did I. The best I thought she'd be able to do would be to match Blaze. I never thought she could beat her. Ebony is reee-eea-ll-y a fast horse."

The morning sun was evaporating the dew, and patches of ground fog were burning off. The air, still cool, smelled fresh and clean. Startled by the horses, a few pheasants scurried across the road.

Sometime later Brad said, "We're getting close to the holdup site, it's just around the next bend."

"Who's that ahead?" asked Audrey.

"I don't know. Let's slow down." They slowed the horses down to a walk and looked at the rider coming toward them.

Audrey spoke first. "It looks like an Indian."

"Yes, and it looks like Running Bear," predicted Brad. As they got closer, Brad confirmed excitedly, "It is Running Bear!"

"Bear, I haven't seen you since last summer!" exclaimed Brad.

Running Bear, or Bear, as his friends called him, halted his horse in front of Brad and Audrey. His horse nickered. Bear answered: "Yes, little one, it has been a long time. What are you doing so far from home?"

Brad told him about the robbery and their visit to the holdup site. "We found some clues too; a bolt, half a plug of chewing tobacco, and a metal toecap from a boot."

Audrey added, "We're going back to the holdup site to look again. It's just around the bend."

Brad continued enthusiastically, "Bear, you're the best tracker in the area. And Pa says the Overland Stage Company is offering a reward for capturing the robbers, or for information that leads to their capture. If we find out who they are, there'll be a two-thousand-dollar reward to split. That's one thousand for you and one thousand for us. Will you help?"

"Yes, I will help," agreed Running Bear. "The reward will help buy new books for our school." Then he smiled. "Or should I say: Running Bear help. Need books for school."

Brad and Audrey laughed. They knew that Running Bear had spent many years at the church's mission school and spoke excellent English. He had even taught English at the Riverton Bible College. At times, however, he teased the youngsters by acting as if he spoke little English.

Brad and Audrey gently nudged their horses forward. Running Bear reined his horse around and came abreast of them. When they reached the site, Brad stopped and said, "This is where we tied our horses yesterday. We'll tell you what we know about the holdup."

Audrey showed him the tree stump and the spot where the bolt had been found. Brad explained how they had searched the downhill side of the road and found the half plug of chewing tobacco. They pointed out the bushes where the robbers had hidden and described their search of the area for clues. Finally,

Brad pointed to the boulder at the crest of the hill where the sharpshooter had hidden.

"Behind the boulder is a clump of trees where they kept their horses," said Brad. "Sheriff Tate tried to follow their trail but lost it after half a mile."

Running Bear studied the crest of the hill for a minute, then said, "Let's go to the top of the hill. The trail they left and the place where their horses were tethered should have much to tell us."

The three led their horses up the steep hill, cutting back and forth through the trees, boulders, and brush until they reached the top. Ebony snorted when she reached the top of the hill. Brad, Audrey, and Running Bear looked down the hill at the road as they regained their breath.

"It is a very good place for an ambush," observed Running Bear. "They planned the robbery very well. Now, let's go to the boulder and think like the sharpshooter." Running Bear talked about the sun, the horses tethered in the clump of trees, the holdup, the warning shot, the climb up the hill with the strongbox, and the ride away from the holdup.

Running Bear continued, "You and Sheriff Tate did not find any food wrappers. The men probably stayed at a cabin or campsite overnight, ate breakfast, rode here, and then robbed the stage. To the north and the west there are only mountains. Riverton is to the south. The men probably went east, where there are ranches. Show me the robbers' tracks."

Brad led Ebony as he walked to the clump of trees. "Here's where the horses were tied. The tracks lead north."

"Follow the tracks, and they will eventually go east," predicted Running Bear.

They mounted their horses and rode single file behind Brad as he followed the robbers' trail. When they reached the rocky area, the trail disappeared. "This is where Sheriff Tate said he lost their trail," said Brad.

"Do you remember how I showed you the way to find a trail?" asked Running Bear as he patiently looked at Brad for the answer.

"Yes. We go to the left and make a big circle. We should find their trail before we complete the circle. If we don't find their trail, we do it again, but with a bigger circle."

"Very good, have you discovered anything else?"

"Yes. One of their horses has large hooves." Brad thought for a moment and then continued, "And, all of the horses are shod."

"Very good, you have learned well." Running Bear turned to Audrey and asked, "And you, Miss Benton, have you discovered anything about the robbers?"

Audrey responded to Running Bear's question, "We've learned quite a bit about the robbers. They probably live in the Riverton area, and at least one of them has worked for a lumber company. One of them probably needs a metal toecap replaced on his boot." Audrey thought for a minute and then continued with an enlightened smile, "And the sharpshooter was probably a soldier in the Civil War."

"And," Brad interjected, "they may have an accomplice in the Denver bank."

Running Bear nodded. "You are good detectives. Let's start the circle and find their trail."

The three mounted their horses and started the circle. Following Running Bear's instructions, they rode about ten feet apart and headed for a reference point. Their first reference point was a large dead pine tree. Their second was a large rock jutting out of the mountainside. On the way to their third reference point, Audrey stopped.

"I think I've found something," said Audrey pointing to part of a deer carcass. "Only the hindquarters were taken. This was done by man, not an animal."

"That is correct, Miss Benton. It was done by a very wasteful man." Running Bear showed anger as he continued, "most hunters, whether a white man or an Indian, would have used the entire deer. The ribs make good stew, and the hide makes clothes. The men who did this only wanted one or two meals. They were in a hurry. They wasted one of God's treasures."

"Here's their trail; they're heading west?" Brad said questioningly, looking at the sun.

"Let's follow their trail west. It will change again," Running Bear predicted.

The three mounted their horses and followed the trail west. After about a mile, the robbers' trail abruptly turned north toward a meadow and entered a small stream. The trail, however, did not resume on the other side of the stream.

"They must have followed the stream to hide their tracks," said Brad. "Now if I were one of the robbers, I'd want anybody tracking me to think I continued north, or west. We should follow the stream north. Is that right, Running Bear?"

"We can follow the stream north, and if we don't find

their trail, we can go south. I'll take the west side of the stream while you and your sister take the east side."

The three followed the stream north. Half a mile farther, Running Bear stopped. "One horse came out here and went north." He followed the trail about 100 feet into a rocky area.

"His trail has disappeared again," said Running Bear as he turned his horse back to the stream. "He probably went back to the stream." Running Bear intently followed the trail for a minute, and then said, "He entered the stream here. He is a careless and lazy man. He entered the stream through the grass where it is easy to follow a trail. He should have entered through the rocks where it would be hard to follow."

Brad and Audrey watched intently as Running Bear followed the horses' tracks back into the stream. Running Bear stopped his horse in the stream and looked at Brad and Audrey. "Only one man came north. The rest of the men went south. We will follow the stream south and find where they left the stream."

They followed the stream south, Brad and Audrey on the east side and Running Bear on the west. They went past the meadow where the robbers had entered the stream. Continuing south about a mile, Audrey saw something on a large rock, stopped her horse and dismounted. She examined some reddish-brown stains on the rock. She moistened her finger with some saliva and rubbed one of the drops. "Running Bear, I think there's some blood on the rock. Probably blood from the deer, am I correct?"

Running Bear crossed the stream and checked one

of the drops. "You are probably correct. Now look to the east, and you will find the trail." He said confidently.

Audrey and Brad slowly circled around the rocky area. "I found it!" shouted Brad. "Here's their trail. There were several horses, and one with big hooves. They didn't even try to hide their trail. They probably didn't think anyone could follow it. And they're heading east, just like you said."

Running Bear crossed the stream and joined Brad and Audrey. The three rode abreast as they followed the trail east. The sun was high in the sky, and the air was still as they drew near a stand of pines. Brad broke the silence and said, "I'm hungry. My stomach keeps telling me that it wants one of Nana's venison sandwiches. How about stopping for lunch when we reach those trees?"

"My stomach's asking me about lunch too," said Audrey. "We have plenty of food, Nana packed the lunches."

Running Bear laughed. "Then we will have a good meal, for Gentle Water also packed one for me."

They stopped when they reached the stand of pines. They dismounted and untied their canteens and the flour sacks with their lunches. Brad and Running Bear hobbled the horses in a grassy area where they could graze next to a small pond.

Audrey sorted out the two lunches that Nana had packed and said, "We have venison sandwiches, apples, apple-blackberry pie, cornbread, and hard-boiled eggs." Looking at Running Bear, she asked, "What did Gentle Water pack for you?"

Running Bear opened a leather pouch and looked at

the contents before answering, "Roast bear, pine nuts, and an apple."

"I've never had bear," said Brad. "I'll give you half a venison sandwich for some of the roast bear."

Audrey added, "I'd like to try some too. Would you like a hardboiled egg?"

"Victoria's venison sandwiches are great. I remember her making them for me when I taught English at the Riverton Bible College." Then Running Bear pulled out a large knife. Quickly he cut the slab of roast bear into bite-sized pieces and then cut Brad's sandwich in half.

"This is greasy, but good!" said Brad as he tasted the roast bear.

Audrey took a piece and remarked, "Yes! The taste is like roast pork, but I like roast pork better."

"None of the bear was wasted; it makes roast, stew, dried meat, moccasins, and fur blankets." Running Bear took half of a venison sandwich. After taking a bite he continued, "Just as I remember. Victoria's venison sandwiches are superb."

The three sat in the shade of the pine trees as they ate. A gentle breeze tempered the heat of the sun. Running Bear put a finger to his lips and pointed to a white tailed deer that had just walked into the clearing. "If you are patient, your prey will move so you can see it, just like the deer. The robbers are our prey. If we are patient, we will find them." Looking back to Brad and Audrey, he continued. "You must not be anxious like most white men. You must be patient. Remember, you found the trail of the robbers that the sheriff could not find. If we are patient, the robbers will move and we can see them."

They finished eating and wrapped their apples for later. Brad tied down his lunch sack and canteen.

"Do you really think we'll find the robbers?" Brad asked Running Bear as they removed the hobbles from horses.

"I don't know, but we have found their trail. We have been patient and followed all the tracks we found. It is likely that we will discover where they went. It may be a ranch, a cabin, or back to Riverton. If they went back to Riverton, we'll give our clues to the sheriff. If their trail leads to a cabin or ranch, we'll be able to lead the sheriff to the cabin or tell him which ranch."

"We'll find them," said Audrey. "We've found their trail, and they aren't trying to hide it any more. They're careless. And just think about what we can do with $1,000."

"The trail we are on leads to the Big Foot Mine," said Running Bear. "The prospector who found the vein of gold talked about seeing some large furry wild men with big feet in the area. He had heard the Indian legend about Big Foot, and said seeing the wild men meant the legend must be true; thus, the name Big Foot Mine. He said large rocks had been thrown at his cabin by Big Foot. When other prospectors came around, he showed them large footprints in the forest. Other prospectors in the area reported that large rocks had also been thrown at them. The rocks were probably thrown by the owner of the Big Foot Mine to scare away the new prospectors. The stories didn't keep men away from the area though; the lure of the gold was too strong. But people remember the legend and fear Big Foot."

"Is there really a Big Foot?" asked Brad.

"I'll tell you more about Big Foot later," said Running Bear. "Now we must follow the trail."

Brad mounted Ebony, waited until Bear and Audrey had mounted, and then said, "Let's go."

Audrey and Running Bear followed Brad as he tracked the robbers' trail through the pine trees. Half an hour later they neared a short rocky hill. Running Bear said, "Let's stop here. I want go to the top of that hill and see what's ahead."

Brad and Audrey waited as Running Bear rode toward the top of the hill. Just before he reached the top, he dismounted and walked, and then crawled to the top of the hill. In a few minutes he climbed down from the highest rock, mounted his horse, and returned.

"There's a cabin ahead. It looks deserted, but we must make sure."

"How do we do that?" asked Audrey. "We don't want to just ride up and knock on the door."

Running Bear smiled and said, "We knock on the roof."

Running Bear selected several rocks the size of a small chicken egg. Quickly he fashioned a leather sling and then practiced throwing the rocks. "David smote Goliath with a sling. I'll knock on the cabin's roof by throwing a rock with this sling. If someone is inside, they'll come out to see what happened."

Brad helped Running Bear select a few more rocks for the sling. Then they followed the trail around the hill and stopped behind some boulders that hid them from the cabin. Running Bear placed a rock in the sling, whirled it and sent it flying toward the cabin. The rock went over the cabin and into the trees. He inserted a second rock and sent it flying toward the cabin. This time the rock hit the roof with a loud crack.

"It must be empty. No one came out," concluded Brad.

"Wait a few minutes," said Running Bear. "We will throw another rock and see if anyone comes out."

A minute later, Running Bear slung another rock on to the roof of the cabin. There was another loud crack. Again, no one came out.

"The cabin is probably empty," said Running Bear. "I will ride up alone and holler them out. You two stay here, out of sight, until I call you. If someone is there," he grinned, "I will be a dumb Indian who saw Big Foot."

CHAPTER 4
THE BIG FOOT MINE

Running Bear rode toward the cabin and hollered, "Anyone home?" There was no response, so he continued, "I am coming in."

He opened the door and entered the cabin. A few seconds later he came back to the door of the cabin and waved for Brad and Audrey to join him.

"Let's go," said Brad as he mounted his horse. Brad guided Ebony through the pines to the trail. Audrey followed him as they both moved their horses to a trot. When they reached the cabin, they stopped beside Running Bear's horse, dismounted, and looped their reins over the small hitching rail.

As they reached the cabin door, Running Bear met them. "Be patient and look carefully. What can you learn from this cabin?" he asked.

Brad and Audrey took a couple of steps into the cabin, stopped, and looked around. The cabin was one large room with some bunks on the left side and a stove on the right. In the center of the cabin were a rectangular table and five chairs. A large, greasy skillet was on the counter under the cabin's only window. A coffeepot with some coffee still in it was on the back of the stove.

"There're the bones from the deer," said Audrey pointing to a couple of bones on the floor by the counter.

Brad went to the stove, took off the cover, and looked inside. Then he carefully stuck his hand into the stove and felt the ashes. "The ashes are still a little warm. They must have used the stove to cook breakfast this morning."

Audrey was examining the counter. "Five cups have been used recently and so have four of the plates." She turned to Running Bear and asked, "Why five cups and four plates?" She paused for a moment before she continued. "The four robbers ate here, and they were met by a fifth person who just had coffee."

"The fifth man was probably the one who knew about the shipment of money," surmised Brad.

"Let's go outside and follow their trail," said Audrey.

"I will take the lead," said Running Bear. "Audrey, you follow me, then Brad."

As they started down the trail, Brad thought, *Running Bear took the lead to protect us in case we meet the robbers. He put Audrey in front of me so I can help her if something happens.*

They followed the narrow trail of the five horses as it twisted through the pine trees, rocks, and brush. A gentle breeze countered the heat as the midday sun slowly moved to their right.

When they came to a clearing, Brad spurred Ebony forward and asked, "Running Bear, are we in danger?"

Running Bear stopped his horse and waited until all of them had stopped before answering. "There is always danger, even at night when you are asleep in your bed.

If I thought we were in danger from the robbers, I would have sent both of you back for help."

"Are we getting close?" asked Brad.

"Yes, we are getting close to the robbers," replied Running Bear. "I believe that they are heading to the Big Foot Mine. It was abandoned five years ago. The mine is about two miles from here. We will be crossing an old mining road that leads to Riverton in a few minutes."

"You're bleeding!" Brad exclaimed, as he saw blood on Audrey's sleeve.

"It's just a small cut from a tree branch," she replied. Then she looked closer and said, "My shirt's torn too, and it's a good-size cut."

They all dismounted so they could examine Audrey's arm. Brad gently pulled the torn shirtsleeve away from the cut. The cut was bleeding very slowly. "You won't die, but we've got to stop the bleeding." He took off his kerchief and pressed it to the wound.

"I will get some moss," said Running Bear as he went into a clump of bushes. A few moments later he emerged with a handful of moss. Brad removed his kerchief, and Running Bear pressed the clump of moss against the wound.

"That should stop the bleeding," said Brad as he wrapped his kerchief around his sister's arm.

"You bandage very well," said Running Bear.

"My father taught me. He said everyone should know how to bandage wounds, but I never thought I'd be bandaging my own sister."

"Ma's going to be angry when she sees my shirt's been torn," said Audrey.

Brad untied his canteen and rinsed the blood off his

hands. After shaking most of the water off, he wiped his hands on his pants. Smiling he said, "Don't worry about Ma. With the reward money you can buy everyone a new shirt."

"Let's move on," said Audrey. "We're almost to the mine. If we find that the robbers did go to the mine, we can go tell the sheriff."

The trees and brush thinned out and the three were able to ride abreast. They crossed the old mining road, and started a gentle climb up the hill toward the abandoned mine.

"We will move off the trail now and go north," said Running Bear. "Then, we can approach the mine from the uphill side. If someone is there, they will not be able to see us."

As they rode north, the trail narrowed, and again they rode single file. About a mile north of the mine, Running Bear raised his hand, and they stopped. He turned in his saddle and held his finger to his lips, then dismounted. Brad and Audrey also dismounted.

"The birds are quiet," whispered Running Bear. "We must listen for a few minutes."

The silence of the forest was broken by a couple of men shouting. Running Bear motioned them to follow him. Hiding behind a clump of bushes, they could see two men in a large clearing about 100 yards ahead.

"I see someone in a costume," warned Running Bear in a very soft voice.

"He's wearing a shaggy wig," whispered Brad. "Now he's putting on some furry boots."

They watched as the man finished putting on the furry black boots, and then a shaggy fur coat.

One of the men shouted, "That's good, Clay. I'm really scared of you. You look like Big Foot."

Big Foot took off the wig and replied, "I bet you'd be afraid if you didn't know it was me."

"Stay still," commanded Running Bear. If they see us, ride as fast as you can to town. Just follow that old mining road. It's about five miles to Riverton."

The man called Clay took off the shaggy fur coat and put it in a large sack. While he was taking off the boots, the other man rode into the meadow with Clay's horse. Clay mounted and the three of them rode down the hill.

"Why would someone want to act like Big Foot?" asked Audrey

"I'll tell you the Indian legend of Big Foot," said Running Bear. "The Indian name for Big Foot is Sasquatch. It means wild man of the forest. Sasquatch lives in the mountains."

Running Bear talked about Big Foot for a few minutes. "But remember that Big Foot is afraid of man, especially the white man. He lives higher in the mountains and likes very rugged country. He would never live this close to man."

"Let's follow them," urged Brad. "If they go to the mine, we'll be able to tell Sheriff Tate where he can find them."

"Since we are so close to the mine, let us see if anyone is there," said Running Bear.

The three rode single file on an old Indian trail toward the mine. In a few minutes, they could see the roof of the mine office in the distance.

"We will leave our horses in these bushes," said Running Bear. They dismounted and tied their horses to the bushes. "Follow me to the top of this hill. We will be able to hide behind those junipers."

They climbed to the top of the hill, crawling the last few feet. Peering through the bushes, Running Bear said, "We can see the mine from here. There are three horses in front of the mine office. What else can you see?"

Brad and Audrey looked at the mining facility for a few minutes. Audrey spoke first. "I see the horse with the large hooves. It looks like part Shire. That's a breed of English draft horses that Pa told me about. He said knights used them in the Middle Ages as war horses. Some Shires were brought to Massachusetts in the 1840s, and now they're used all through the country."

"Look, some men are coming out of the mine," said Brad.

Three men left the mine and mounted the horses. From their hiding place in the junipers, Brad, Audrey, and Running Bear could hear what the men were saying.

"We'll go back to the ranch and see what the boss has heard," said the man called Clay.

One of the other men replied, "Yeah, and get a real meal. If we hadn't shot that doe, we'd be out of beans by now."

"We'll come back tomorrow and finish up," said Clay. He spurred his horse into a gallop, and the other two men did the same. In a minute they were out of sight.

"Wow!" exclaimed Brad. "They must be the robbers. They said they shot the deer. But what ranch are they going to?"

"Probably the Big Foot," said Running Bear. "The owner of the Big Foot mine bought the Bar-H and renamed it the Big Foot ranch when the vein of gold petered out."

"The Big Foot," questioned Brad, "where's that?"

"There is a fork about two miles south on the road to Riverton. Take the east fork, and you will have about a five-mile ride to the Big Foot ranch. Go straight, and it is three miles to Riverton."

"I'll go to town for the sheriff," said Audrey.

Brad looked at his sister's bloody shirt and said, "That's not safe. I'll ride with you to the fork. If you feel okay, you can go on to Riverton alone and I'll come back and stay with Running Bear."

"I feel fine," said Audrey. "But if you insist, you can ride with me to the fork."

"Go back the way we came," said Running Bear. "When you reach the road, take it to Riverton. Do not go through the mining camp on the way to Riverton. When the robbers return, we want them to see only their tracks, not ours."

Audrey and Brad mounted their horses and followed the trail back to the road. Brad looked carefully at his sister.

"Brad, I'm fine. You really don't have to go with me."

"You're probably right, but I did promise Running Bear that I'd go with you to the fork. Besides, if we meet the robbers, I can lead them away from you while you get the sheriff."

"We won't meet the robbers," said Audrey. "They've gone to the Big Foot Ranch." Audrey thought a minute and then continued. "Do you really think they're the robbers? I'm excited, but I'm also scared. If they are the robbers and they see us, we could be in danger."

"We're just two kids out for a ride," said Brad. "They won't bother us."

Audrey laughed, "You're right. They might even tell us about Big Foot. If they do that, we'll scream and ride into town as fast as we can."

Brad and Audrey looked at the abandoned mines and their tailings that scarred the hillsides. The mineshafts resembled giant gopher holes. The Big Foot Mine's long vein of gold had attracted numerous prospectors. Those hopeful prospectors had staked claims and dug into the hillside looking for a large vein of gold like the Big Foot vein. None of them found any gold, and they abandoned their claims. Now, the mines were only ugly sores on a beautiful mountain.

Looking down the trail, Audrey glanced to the sun on her right and said, "I see the fork to the east. I'll continue on the main road to Riverton."

"There's the sign that points to the Big Foot," said Brad. "Running Bear's memory of the area is perfect."

"Brad thanks for riding with me. I'll get Pa and the sheriff and bring them back as fast as I can. Go back to Running Bear."

Audrey nudged Blaze to a lope and headed toward Riverton. Brad watched his sister for a few moments. Then he reined Ebony around and quickly brought his horse to a fast trot as he headed back to join Running Bear.

Sheriff Tate shrugged his shoulders and opened his hands in frustration. "I'm sorry; Harold, but I don't have any new information about the robbery."

Harold Benton replied, "I know you're trying, Richard. I just thought that maybe some additional clues might have turned up."

Mr. Benton left the sheriff and headed toward the stage office. He felt frustrated about the robbery and thought, *it would be nice if Brad and Audrey found some new clues. The sheriff's stumped. He's investigated many crimes, and he usually solves them. But we've found very few clues on this robbery. Well, I must be patient. Some additional clues are bound to turn up.*

Meanwhile, Audrey gently leaned forward in her saddle as she entered the outskirts of Riverton. Blaze had enjoyed the lope from the Big Foot Mine. Moments later, entering Main Street, Audrey pulled Blaze back to a comfortable trot. Two elderly ladies stopped talking and watched her ride down the street.

Harold Benton heard a horse coming up behind him at a trot. He started turning to see who was riding into town, but was interrupted in mid-turn by the voice of his daughter.

"Pa!" yelled Audrey, as she halted Blaze beside her father. Quickly dismounting, she looped her reins over the rail and dashed to her father.

"Audrey!" said her father. "What are you doing here?"

"We found the robbers!" she exclaimed. "Let's get the sheriff!"

"Slow down, Miss Pinkerton," said her father. "Tell me more about what you found as we go to the sheriff's office, and make it a very short story. But, where is Brad?"

As they walked to the sheriff's office, Audrey related what she and Brad had discovered. "We found their trail about three miles from the holdup site. We followed it to a cabin where they stayed after the robbery and were met by a fifth man. The robbers left the cabin this morning and went to the Big Foot Mine. And one of them has a Big Foot costume. Brad and Running Bear are in the forest behind the mine now."

"That was a very short story. Now tell me how Running Bear got involved."

"We met him on the trail. We told him about the reward and asked him if he could help us. He said he would; he'll use the reward to buy new books for his school."

Sheriff Tate stood in the doorway of his office. Looking at Audrey and her father, he smiled and said, "I thought you'd be back. When I saw Audrey riding down the street at a trot, I knew she'd found something. So, Audrey, what did you discover?"

Audrey related how they had found the robbers' trail and followed it to the cabin. Sheriff Tate expressed surprise when she told him about the Big Foot costume and the men going to the mine. He opened his mouth when she told him that Brad and Running Bear were waiting in the forest behind the mine for him and a posse.

"I don't doubt what you've told me. It certainly looks like you've discovered the robbers. But, before I can arrest them, I'll need more evidence. I hope we find that evidence at the mine."

"Audrey, you're hurt!" exclaimed her father, finally noticing his daughter's bandaged arm.

"It's just a cut from a tree branch. Brad and Running

Bear fixed it. Running Bear put some moss on it and Brad tied it up with his kerchief. It doesn't hurt."

"Do you feel well enough to take your Pa and me to your brother and Bear?" asked the sheriff.

"We'll need more than you and Pa," said Audrey. "There were five of them at the cabin. Three rode away from the mine and went to the Big Foot Ranch."

"You're right about needing more men," said the sheriff. "Were there any men at the mine when you left?"

"All the horses were gone when Brad and I left the mine. It's possible some men were still there. If someone is still there, he's inside the mine and without a horse."

Sheriff Tate picked up his rifle and said, "Harold, I'll go to the livery stable and get our horses. On the way, I'll get five or six men to deputize. On the way to the stage office, you can get some good men, too. Tell them we'll meet here in ten minutes. Don't tell anyone what I need them for. If there's an inside man in Riverton, we don't want to tip our hand." Then, with a mischievous grin, he continued, "If they ask, tell them we think Brad's been kidnapped. They'd best bring a jacket too. We might be out all night."

Harold Benton, looking at his daughter's bandaged arm and sweat-streaked face, said, "Audrey, go next door to Doc Adams and have him look at your arm. Be sure to tell him he has only ten minutes before you have to be back at the sheriff's office and on your horse."

"I'll hurry," said Audrey.

Audrey went next door to see Doc Adams, climbed the stairs to the second floor and entered his office.

"Audrey Benton," greeted Mrs. Adams, "I haven't seen you for some time. What can I do for you?"

"I'd like your husband to look at my arm. I got a bad cut from a tree branch."

"I'm sorry, Audrey, but he left an hour ago to help Mrs. Simpson deliver a baby. He won't be back till late tonight, maybe not even until tomorrow night. Come over to the exam table, and I'll take a look at it."

Audrey went to the table with Mrs. Adams. As she started to remove the kerchief, Audrey said, "I haven't got much time. I have to be back at the sheriff's office and on my horse in a few minutes. Sheriff Tate and Pa are getting deputies now to help find my brother. The sheriff thinks he's been kidnapped."

Mrs. Adams finished removing the bandage and looked at the cut. "This is going to hurt," she said applying a solution of carbolic acid to the wound.

Audrey winced as the solution touched the wound. "The cut's not too deep," said Mrs. Adams. "I'll put on a little salve and a clean bandage. Why, in a few days you'll be as good as new. Now you better get going, so you can get to the sheriff's office on time."

Audrey rushed to the door and grasped the doorknob. Pausing for a moment, she turned around and said, "Thanks, Mrs. Adams."

Audrey ran down the steps and toward the sheriff's office to get her horse. Some men were already gathering outside the office. She saw her father coming out of the stage office in the next block with his jacket in his left hand and his rifle in his right. Pulling the reins off the hitching rail, she mounted her horse. "Come on, Blaze. Let's give Pa a ride." She reined to the left, gave a gentle squeeze, and guided Blaze toward her father.

"Audrey, we're supposed to meet at the sheriff's office, not the stage office."

"I know, but I thought you might like to ride there." Audrey smiled, "Come on, Pa, climb up behind me."

A big grin spread over his face as he put his foot in the stirrup, grabbed the saddle horn, and swung up behind his daughter. "It has been a hard day, and it is a long block to the sheriff's office. What did Doc Adams say about your arm?"

"He's out helping Mrs. Simpson deliver her baby. Mrs. Adams looked at the cut. She put carbolic acid and a salve on it, and then she put on a new bandage. It should be okay in a few days."

Sheriff Tate arrived at his office the same time as Audrey and her father. He stopped his horse and held out the reins of Harold's horse. "Here's your horse, Harold. I got six men for the posse. Four are already here. How'd you do?"

Audrey's father dismounted Blaze and said, "I got five men. Sam and Jake are already here. Jim Bates and Hank Lacy will be here in a minute. Hank sent one of his men ahead to the Bar-X for some additional help. He'll meet us at the fork to the Bar-X."

The sheriff looked at the men outside his office. That's one of the things he liked about Riverton. These good citizens always helped each other. This time, as in the past, men had volunteered without knowing what was needed. They knew that when he asked for a posse, it was possible that the some of them could be hurt or killed. Still, he had no trouble getting volunteers.

"Okay, men. Let's go inside, and I'll deputize you," said the sheriff.

"We're with you, Sheriff," said Hank Lacy. "I sent one of my men back to the ranch for some help. He'll meet us at the fork to the Bar-X with some more men."

The men crowded into the sheriff's office. Sheriff Tate opened his drawer and brought out a box of badges. "Everyone take a badge and put it on. Same goes for you two men just coming in. Before I swear you boys in, I'm laying down some rules. No one leaves the posse or talks to anyone after I swear you in. If you have to say good-bye to someone before we leave, it's too late. I can't use you as a deputy. We're together from this point on. Anyone have to leave?"

"We're all with you, Richard," said Hank Lacy as he looked at the men. "No one will say another word until we meet my men from the Bar-X."

"Everyone agrees to that?" asked the sheriff. There was chorus of agreement from the men.

"If that's your rule, so be it," declared Jake Jackson. "My wife said you needed me worse than she did. Besides, I don't like spring cleaning."

There was a roar of laughter, and a man in the back of the room hollered, "I don't blame you Jake; I'd rather be on Tate's posse than do spring cleaning."

"All right men, raise your right hands." The twelve men enthusiastically raised their right hands. Sheriff Tate had them repeat the oath and pin on their badges.

"Men, Audrey, it's time to mount up," said the sheriff.

Some wives were outside the sheriff's office with bags of food and canteens of water to give their husbands as they emerged. Since some of the women had packed two or three bags of food, there was at least one bag of food and a canteen of water for everyone. Jake Jackson's wife gave Audrey and her father each a bag of food and a canteen of water. The men tied their jackets behind their saddles or stuffed them into their saddlebags. Audrey and her father were at the front of the posse with the sheriff's horse.

Sheriff Tate mounted his horse and looked at the posse. He knew time was precious and that Brad and Running Bear were waiting for him. "Let's go, men. I'll tell you more at the fork to the Bar-X."

Audrey and her father gently moved their horses to a fast trot. The sheriff and the posse followed behind them.

CHAPTER 5
RUNNING BEAR IS CAPTURED

"The posse should arrive in about an hour," Brad said optimistically. He stared into the forest for a minute and then asked, "Bear, when do you think they'll get here?"

Running Bear looked down the mountain toward Riverton and rubbed his chin. "It will be at least an hour and a half from now."

"The birds to our left must have talked themselves out," said Brad. "They're quiet now."

"Or someone is coming this way," said Running Bear. "We should separate. Go into that thicket and do not make a sound. I will act as if I am looking for you."

Brad untethered Ebony and led her through a narrow opening in a thicket of blackberries and into a clump of trees. He tied a rawhide strip around her muzzle to keep her from nickering. Then, he carefully crawled into the blackberry bushes and hid.

Running Bear cupped his hands around his mouth and yelled, "Brad!" Then he got on his horse and rode away from Brad and down a small draw before he yelled Brad's name again. He came back from the draw and rode to the top of a little knoll, cupped his hands, and again yelled Brad's name.

70

"All right, Injun, hold it right there," commanded a man behind Bear. "Get down from your horse, real slow, and no sudden moves."

Running Bear did as he was ordered. He slowly turned to see who had given the order. The man was pointing a Henry rifle at him. Running Bear asked the man, "I am looking for a boy who was hunting with me. Have you seen him?"

"I ain't seen anyone except you, and you're on private property," the man said menacingly. "What's your name?"

"Running Bear; I did not know this was private property. I saw no signs or fences."

"Well, everyone knows this is the property of the Big Foot Mining Co. We'll go talk to the boss. Get back on your horse."

Running Bear mounted his horse as ordered and started down the narrow trail to the mine. The man followed, holding the rifle in his right hand.

Brad watched from the thicket as Running Bear and the man with the rifle went down the trail toward the mine.

After waiting a few minutes, Brad quietly left the thicket and returned to the secluded overlook. He watched the man and Running Bear dismount and enter the mine. A few minutes later, two men left the mine. The man with the rifle mounted his horse, and another man got on Running Bear's horse. Then the two men rode out of the mine yard. When they reached the road, they turned north, away from Riverton.

Brad thought to himself, *they'll find where we crossed the road and follow the trail to me. But, they'll never think of looking for me in the mine. Besides, I have to see what they did with Running Bear. He let himself be captured so I could stay free.*

Brad went back to the dense clump of young trees for Ebony. He led her into the clearing, mounted her, and rode down the trail to the mine. Just before he reached the mine yard, he stopped, dismounted and put on his jacket.

Brad quickly picked a few red berries, and used their juice to write something on the saddle. Then he tied the reins to the saddle horn and said, "It's time to send you for help, Ebony. I hope you meet Audrey and Blaze on the road," and then he gave her a whack on the rump. Ebony immediately broke into a run, went through the mine yard to the road, and headed toward Riverton.

Staying under the trees and within the underbrush, Brad moved toward the mine entrance. He quickly moved between bushes and abandoned mining equipment until he reached a couple of broken ore carts near the entrance to the mine. He asked himself, *how do I overcome a man with a gun?*

One of the ore carts had some hand tools, picks, axes, small tree limbs, and shovels. Brad picked up a small tree limb, about 4 feet long, and gave it a couple of practice swings. *If I'm going to help Running Bear, I'd better get going.*

He dashed into the mine and stopped. Listening carefully, he waited for his eyes to adjust to the darkness. The air was dank and musty. He could hear someone talking, but he couldn't understand what was being said. Slowly, he crept deeper into the mine. Rounding a bend in the mineshaft, he could see a light.

He stopped and listened. He could hear voices, and one of them was Running Bear's.

"Zeke, there are many beasts which you call Big Foot," said Running Bear. "Indians call them Sasquatch. They avoid man, but they are not afraid of man. If angered, they will attack and kill. I saw two Sasquatch capture a renegade Indian who had shot at them."

"What happened to the renegade?" Zeke asked. His eyes opened wide with fear.

"I never saw him again," replied Running Bear.

Brad slowly inched toward the light and the voices. Running Bear was in an enlarged area of the mineshaft, his hands and feet tied with rope. Running Bear saw Brad, but continued talking with Zeke.

Zeke was of average build and a little under six feet tall. A hat covered his dark brown hair. His rifle leaned against a crate a few feet away from the box on which he sat. He leaned forward, listening intently to Running Bear talk about Big Foot.

"Sasquatch likes caves," said Running Bear. "If he comes into the mine, we won't have a chance. If we wait for your boss outside in the mine office, we'll be safe."

"Your feet are tied, Injun, but you can take short steps," said Zeke. "Get up real slow, and let's go to the office."

Running Bear scraped his boots noisily on the mine floor as he tried to stand up. Brad took a long step behind Zeke and swung the tree limb. A muffled thwack sounded as the limb hit Zeke. The blow was softened by the hat and the tip of the limb broke when it struck Zeke. Despite this, Zeke crumpled to the floor, motionless.

"Bear, I'm glad you're all right," said Brad as he

unsheathed a small knife and cut the ropes binding Running Bear's hands.

"Slade and Clay are out looking for you," said Running Bear. "Let's tie up Zeke and get ready for their return."

They quickly used some ropes to tie Zeke's hands and feet and then propped him up against the crate where Running Bear had been a few minutes earlier. Running Bear removed Zeke's hat and put his own hat on Zeke, pulling it down over Zeke's face. Next, he stuffed Zeke's pistol into his belt and then hid Zeke's rifle behind some crates.

"Zeke's a little shorter than you, Bear, but you're both wearing brown shirts and dark blue pants," said Brad examining Zeke. "It looks like you're taking a nap."

"That is good," said Bear. "When his partners come back, they will see the 'Injun' he was guarding."

"That takes care of one of the robbers. How do we capture the other two?"

"We let them come to us," said Running Bear. "Then, we divide and conquer. Take your broken club and come with me."

Running Bear picked up the lantern, and they looked around the mine. There were several side shafts, some of which were interconnected. Some of the side shafts were only a few feet long; others were much longer. Old ore carts, boxes, and tools were scattered throughout the mine.

"I hear voices; someone's coming into the mine," whispered Brad.

"Put the lantern back on the crate," directed Running Bear. They returned to the open area and placed the lantern back on the empty crate. Running Bear picked up a coil of rope and, motioning Brad to follow him, said, "Now, let us go further into the mine."

They went down a shaft that had many connecting side shafts. Brad scrunched into a short side shaft behind a broken ore cart. Running Bear picked up several rocks and hid in a connecting shaft.

"Slade, Zeke's gone, and the Injun's asleep in the corner," said Clay.

Clay was a hawk-faced lanky man about five feet eight inches tall. He had black hair and gray eyes, and walked with a slight limp. Slade was a short, heavy-set man with brown hair and green eyes. His manner was mean and nasty, but he was very protective of Clay.

"He's probably back in the mine looking for gold," said Slade. "Zeke's always had gold fever."

Running Bear took a rock and threw it back into the black depths of the mineshaft. There was a clatter as the rock bounced off the sides of the shaft.

"Hear that, Clay?" Slade motioned to the dark shaft. "Zeke's farther back in the mine. Let's go see what he's doing."

Slade picked up a couple of unlit lanterns and shook them. "These are full," he said. He struck a match from the box beside the lit lantern. The match flared and then settled into a steady flame. With his left hand he raised the glass and lit the wicks on the two lanterns.

"Here's yours," said Slade as he handed a glowing lantern to Clay.

"I'll stay behind ya," said Clay as he followed Slade into the mine.

"Yeah, stay behind me."

"Is it true 'bout Big Foot likin' caves?" asked Clay.

"There ain't no such thing as a Big Foot. That's just an old Injun tale."

"Well, I'd just as soon stay behind ya'," said Clay.

"Zeke!" shouted Slade. "We're back. Stop lookin' for gold and come help us find that kid."

"Clay, you take the shaft to the right, I'll take the one to the left. Tell Zeke I want him back here now. No more of this huntin' for gold. We've got to find that kid."

Clay timidly walked down the shaft toward Brad. Running Bear stepped out of his hiding place and hit Clay's jaw with a powerful punch. Brad rushed forward and grabbed the lantern before it hit the mine floor. Clay tottered a moment and then collapsed into Running Bear's arms.

Brad began tying Clay's feet and whispered, "Audrey should be getting here with the sheriff any time now."

"Always prepare for the worst," said Running Bear as he finished tying Clay's hands. "When you are prepared for the worst, there is only happiness when the best happens."

"Is that an Indian saying?" asked Brad.

"No, that is based on the Bible, Genesis 41. Joseph said God revealed to the Pharaoh that there would be seven years of feast followed by seven years of famine. The Pharaoh wisely followed Joseph's explanation of the dream and prepared for famine. If we prepare for a famine, we are ready for famine. If there is a feast instead of a famine, we will be pleased."

"So we should act as if Audrey isn't bringing the sheriff?" replied Brad.

"That is correct; we will be ready whether she brings

the sheriff to us or we take Zeke and his partners to the sheriff."

"Now we get Slade," said Brad.

"No. We let Slade come to us." Running Bear picked up another rock and tossed it down a side shaft. Then, he let out a long groan.

"Zeke! Clay!" shouted Slade. "Ya okay?"

Running Bear held his finger to his lips, and then turned off Clay's lantern. The mineshaft was dark. There was a glow of light from the large area where Zeke was tied up. The glow from Slade's lantern increased as he came toward Brad and Running Bear.

Brad felt alone and whispered, "Running Bear." Silence was his only answer. Brad scrunched back behind the ore cart and was very still.

The light from Slade's lantern got brighter and suddenly, a large hand grabbed Brad's jacket and yanked him up.

"I found 'im, Clay," said Slade. "I got the kid."

Slade shoved Brad against the side of mineshaft. "I suppose your name's Brad. Is 'at right, kid?"

"Yes, sir, my name is Brad. Please don't let Big Foot get me. He got your friend."

"There ain't no such thing as a Big Foot," said Slade. "Big Foot is just an old Injun legend. Now where's Clay?"

"He was grabbed by Big Foot. I was hiding from Big Foot when your friend found me. Just as I started to get up so we could leave, Big Foot grabbed him."

"Now, listen kid, there ain't no such thing as Big Foot. Let's go."

"Sure, mister," replied Brad. "But please don't let Big Foot get me. He's big and he really stinks."

There was a loud splat as Running Bear's fist hit Slade's jaw. Again, Brad grabbed the lantern before it hit the floor.

"So Slade does not believe in Big Foot," said Running Bear. "Perhaps we can change his mind."

Sheriff Tate's posse reached the fork to the Bar-X. The road to the ranch, really a wagon trail, went through a few small stands of pine trees. A large board with "Bar-X" burned in it hung between two very large pine trees that straddled the trail. The snowcapped mountains in the distance framed the ranch house, corral and outbuildings.

"That sure is a pretty scene," said Sheriff Tate. "Are you describing the scenery or the six Bar-X hands, Richard?" asked Harold Benton.

"I was talking about the scenery, but the six hands look mighty pretty too."

"Sheriff Tate, Mr. Lacy," said Sam Burnes. "We're ready. We brought some extra food, water and a couple of jackets. I brought the pinto too, in case a horse gets lame."

"Men," said the sheriff, "I've always leveled with you. Here's what we're facing." He nodded toward Audrey and said, "Audrey Benton, her brother Brad, and Running Bear picked up the trail of the stagecoach robbers and followed it to the Big Foot Mine. Brad and Running Bear sent Audrey to get me and a posse. If the men they tracked are the bandits, one of them is a sharpshooter."

There was a quick discussion among the men in the posse. "We're still with ya', Sheriff. Thanks for tellin' us what we're up against. I'm a sharpshooter too, Union Army," shouted Jake Jackson from the back of the posse.

"I'm a sharpshooter too. Confederate Army," said Tom Shadden.

Sheriff Tate smiled and said, "I hope we don't have to use your sharpshooting skills, but I'm pleased to have them."

"We've had a little rustling over the last few years," said Hank Lacy. "The men at the Big Foot Ranch have never been sociable like the rest of the folks in the Riverton area. They've kept to themselves and even threatened our men at times. I've suspected they were rustling some of our cattle, but I never had any proof. It wouldn't surprise me if they're the ones that robbed the stagecoach."

"Doesn't matter whether it's rustlin' or robbin'." said Jake. "A thief's a thief, and stealin' is stealin'."

The distant sound of a galloping horse brought conversation to a halt. The posse looked north toward the sound.

"It's coming fast and without a rider," said the sheriff.

The riderless horse galloped down the road toward the posse. Everyone was silent as they watched the approaching horse.

"It's Ebony!" shouted Audrey breaking the silence. "It's Brad's horse!"

Hank Lacy spurred his horse from the group and galloped out to meet Ebony. Hank pulled his horse to a halt and shouted something that the posse couldn't understand. Ebony instantly slowed to a walk, came to

Hank and stopped. Hank's horse rubbed muzzles with Ebony and nickered.

Sheriff Tate shook his head as Hank brought Ebony over to the posse. "I know you're good with horses, Hank, but I've never seen anyone stop a runaway horse that fast. How did you do it?"

"Simple," said Hank with a big grin. "I broke Ebony to the saddle, and my horse is her mother. I had two very important things going for me."

The men in the posse laughed. "Your secret's out," said Jake Jackson.

Audrey had dismounted and was examining Ebony. "Brad's jacket and his lunch bag are missing," she said. "And there's some writing on his saddle."

Harold Benton looked down at the saddle and said, "It looks like Brad wrote a note on the saddle. RB – COT -- BFM."

"Running Bear's been caught! Big Foot Mine!" exclaimed Audrey.

"I hope Brad is all right," said Harold Benton. "We'll know when we get to the mine."

"Keep a sharp eye, men," ordered Sheriff Tate. "We don't want to be surprised if the men at the mine are the robbers. And don't take any unnecessary risks. I don't want anyone hurt. Let's go."

Sheriff Tate reined his horse toward the mine and headed off at a lope. The sixteen men in the posse did the same. The men rode two and three abreast up the road toward the mine. Audrey followed with Brad's horse.

"We've got the three of them tied up," said Brad. "How do we get them to the sheriff?"

"How many plates at the cabin," asked Running Bear?

Brad smiled weakly and answered, "Four. We've got one more outlaw to capture. We'll wait for him to come to us."

"We will wait for him or the sheriff. Let us find out more about the holdup while we wait. We can drag the men farther down the mine shaft and talk about Big Foot."

Running Bear grabbed Slade under the arms and dragged him down a side shaft of the mine with a vertical airshaft. Then he did the same with Clay and Zeke. The airshaft admitted a small stream of sunlight. Running Bear looped some ropes over Brad's hands and feet. Zeke was starting to come around as Running Bear looped some rope over his own hands and feet and sat down close to the main mine shaft.

"Running Bear, what is Big Foot going to do with us?" asked Brad.

"I do not know; but Big Foot thinks this mine is his. He hit Zeke and tied him up. I was already tied up. How did Big Foot catch you?"

"I was going to leave the mine with the man called Clay, when Big Foot hit him and took him away. I was hiding behind an ore cart when Mr. Slade found me. We started to leave the mine when Big Foot hit him. Then he tied us up and brought us here."

Brad could see Zeke starting to pull frantically at the ropes that bound his hands and feet.

"Is it true that Big Foot eats men who enter his cave?" Brad asked anxiously.

"Yes," explained Running Bear. "Big Foot does not know this is a mine. He thinks it is a cave, his cave. Big Foot thinks we have invaded his home. We may never get out alive."

"Running Bear, you're telling me that Big Foot knocked me out and tied me up?" uttered Zeke.

"Yes, just like he did to your two friends and Brad."

"I've gotta get loose," said Zeke.

Seeing Zeke's anxiety, Brad decided to help increase his fear. "I hope you can get loose, Zeke. If Big Foot gets hurt and doesn't come back to the mine, we could be here forever."

"I've gotta get loose!" exclaimed Zeke pulling frantically at the ropes.

"And if he does come back to the mine, we're just a meal," said Brad.

Zeke, realizing the futility of his struggle, asked hopefully, "Does Big Foot like money?"

"Big Foot does like gold and silver coins and jewelry," replied Running Bear. "An old Indian legend tells about Big Foot exchanging a warrior for some silver jewelry."

"Do you speak Big Foot language?" asked Brad; "at least enough so you can talk to him?"

"All Indians speak some Big Foot," replied Running Bear.

"Could you tell Big Foot I can give him some gold coins if he sets us free?" asked Zeke.

"It would take many gold coins to set us free," said Running Bear.

"How many do you think it would take?" asked Zeke.

"More than any of us have."

"Could you at least ask him?" begged Zeke.

"I can ask Big Foot to take Brad to get the gold coins. If Brad leads him to them, and Big Foot thinks they are enough, he might come back and release us."

"How much gold has he taken to free a man in the past?" asked Zeke anxiously.

"A warrior was released for a bag of silver jewelry," replied Running Bear. "Big Foot would want many bags of gold coins to release all of us. He'd probably want a bag of gold for each of us. It would be many thousands of dollars. We do not have that many gold coins. We might as well accept our fate."

"I know where there are many thousands of dollars in gold coins," said Zeke as he tugged at his ropes again. "That might be enough to buy our freedom," encouraged Running Bear. "If you tell Brad how to find them, Big Foot might let Brad take him to the gold coins."

"Once he gets the gold, how do I know Brad'll come back and free us?"

"How do I know you'll tell me where to find the gold coins?" retorted Brad. "If you give me bad directions, Big Foot will get real angry at me."

"It is our only way out," said Running Bear. "Tell Brad where to take Big Foot for the gold, and we might be set free. If you do not tell him, we can await our fate with Big Foot."

"Listen! Someone's coming," whispered Brad.

"It is Big Foot," whispered Running Bear in reply.

Running Bear started chanting to the imaginary Big Foot. Brad recognized that the chant was in Running Bear's native language.

"Zeke," said Brad, "I sure hope Big Foot wants the gold. I'm too young to be his dinner."

"Is he really talking to Big Foot?" asked Zeke. "It sounds to me like he's just doin' some ol' Injun chant."

"Of course it's an Indian chant. The Indian chant is how he speaks to Big Foot."

Continuing to chant, Running Bear stood up. Brad and the darkness prevented Zeke from seeing what was happening. Running Bear held his "tied" hands in front of his body and scraped his boots on the floor.

"Brad. What's happening?" asked Zeke.

"Big Foot's taking Running Bear farther down the shaft," explained Brad.

That's good! Big Foot must be listening to Running Bear's chant," said Zeke hopefully.

The chanting stopped and was followed by some grunts. Then there was silence, some chanting, and more grunts. Then total silence.

"I don't want to be eaten, Zeke. Tell me how to find the gold," Brad pleaded tearfully.

"Okay kid. Here's how ya' find the gold, so listen carefully."

Zeke described where the money from the robbery was hidden. He had Brad repeat the directions several times to assure that he knew how to find the gold.

"I sure hope Running Bear is successful," said Brad.

After few more minutes of silence, Running Bear came back to Brad and Zeke.

"You can go get the gold, Brad," said Running Bear rubbing his wrists. "Big Foot will free us for the gold coins. Did Zeke give you the directions?"

"Yes, and he even had me repeat the directions five times to be sure," said Brad.

"How come you're untied?" asked Zeke.

"Big Foot untied me after I did the Big Foot chant. Now we have to go with Big Foot to get the gold. I hope you gave Brad good directions. If we do not find the gold, Big Foot will be very angry with us."

"I gave Brad good directions," assured Zeke. "Don't forget that we're still hog-tied. Come back and untie us."

"We will come back with Big Foot and untie you after we give him the gold," confirmed Running Bear.

"Hurry up," said Zeke, "I want to get out of here before that big furry thing changes his mind."

Brad and Running Bear went to the open area where the lanterns and other supplies were stored. Brad picked up the lit lantern. Running Bear selected a second lantern and lit it.

"I'm taking my broken tree limb too," declared Brad. "We might meet one of Zeke's partners."

Together they cautiously started toward the mine entrance.

CHAPTER 6
THE POSSE SAVES THE ROBBERS

The posse entered the yard of the Big Foot Mining Company. Two horses were tied to the hitching post in front of the office. The posse reined their horses to a stop and dismounted. Sheriff Tate and a couple of men with rifles approached the mine entrance. Hank Lacy and his men were already checking out the mine office. Harold Benton and some men were searching the rest of the yard. The two sharpshooters, Jake Jackson and Tom Shadden, were riding to the rock bluff overlooking the mine yard.

"Hank!" shouted Sheriff Tate. "Have a couple of your men bring some lanterns from the manager's office. Let's go into the mine."

Hank Lacy and two of his men waited at the entrance with Sheriff Tate. Two Bar-X men went to the office and brought four lanterns to the sheriff.

"I see a light coming this way," whispered Hank. "You men get behind those ore carts. The sheriff and I'll flank the entrance."

Running Bear and Brad cautiously approached the mine exit. "Running Bear," whispered Brad as he lowered his lantern and grasped the Indian's arm,

86

"Stop, I see some horses. They're either the posse's or the outlaws'."

"I can see four horses," said Running Bear, "three bays and a gray. What do you see?"

"I see a black too," said Brad. "I'm not sure, but it may be Ebony."

Sheriff Tate edged into the entrance of the mine, his back flattened against the side of the shaft and shouted, "You men in the mine, this is Sheriff Tate. Come out with your hands up."

"Audrey made it," said Brad as he squeezed Running Bear's arm. "We're safe."

"Sheriff Tate, this is Brad Benton. Running Bear and I are coming out."

"Lower your weapons," ordered the sheriff, "that's Brad."

Brad and Running Bear lifted their lanterns and hurried to the mine exit. The fresh air replaced the dank atmosphere as they neared the mine entrance. Brad and Running Bear squinted at the bright sunlight as they left the mine.

"Brad, you're all right!" exclaimed Harold Benton as he put an arm around his son.

Audrey ran to Running Bear and gave him a hug. "I'm glad you weren't hurt, Bear. Brad's note on Ebony's saddle said you had been caught."

"Just as Brad's message said, I was captured by the men who robbed the stage. However, Brad rescued me. We have three of the robbers tied up inside the mine. I will let Brad tell you the rest of the story. Then, we will need your posse to catch the other robbers."

"Sounds like you two have been mighty busy,"

observed the sheriff regaining his composure. "Okay, Brad, tell me the rest of the story."

"After Audrey left to get you, Running Bear and I heard someone coming. I hid Ebony in a clump of trees and then crawled into a blackberry thicket and hid, too."

Brad continued telling about the man called Clay capturing Running Bear. "When I saw two men come out of the mine and ride north, one of them using Running Bear's horse, that's when I wrote the message on my saddle and sent Ebony toward Riverton. I couldn't leave Running Bear to the robbers, so I went into the mine to find him. I knew that would be the last place the robbers would expect to find me. Running Bear was tied up, and Zeke was guarding him. So, I used a tree limb to knock out Zeke. Then we captured the robbers called Clay and Slade; I don't know their last names. Later we convinced Zeke that Big Foot had captured all of us. Clay and Slade are still unconscious."

"Big Foot!" exclaimed Hank. "That's just an old Indian Legend. No one's ever seen Big Foot in this area."

"Very true," replied Running Bear, "but the robbers don't know that. They believe that Big Foot has them tied up for trespassing in his cave. Zeke is afraid that Big Foot will eat him. He even told Brad where to find the gold, which we believe is from the stage robbery. Brad and I will be taking Big Foot to a cabin to get the gold. In exchange for gold, Big Foot will free all of us."

There was a roar of laughter from the posse. As the laughter subsided, Jake Jackson said, "You two must be some storytellers, if'n you got those three men to believe in Big Foot."

Sheriff Tate turned to Hank Lacy and said, "Take some men and go rescue the robbers. Tell them you were out looking for Brad, and saw some horses outside the mine. Ask them what they're doing all tied up in an abandoned mine. Don't untie them right away. Let them sweat a little. I want them to believe that they're very lucky that you found them, otherwise Big Foot would have had them for dinner."

"Good idea," said Hank. "I'll let them know that Big Foot likes to store his dinner in caves. If we work it right, they just might confess."

Hank Lacy put up his hand, a mischievous gleam in his eye. He smiled and turned to Running Bear and said, "We should be able to benefit from this Big Foot story. Is that okay with you, Running Bear?"

A slow smile spread across his face as Running Bear replied, "Yes, a very scared boy and a terrified Injun. We know that Big Foot will come back for dinner if he does not get his gold."

Hank and Running Bear laughed and slapped each other on the back.

"I don't know what you two have in mind, and I don't think I want to know," said the sheriff with a big smile.

"Sam," said Hank. "Let's go save those three robbers from Big Foot. The rest of you men wait here for us."

"Good," said the sheriff, "I'll take Running Bear, the Bentons, and a couple of men with me to the cabin for the gold."

"Running Bear, you're without a horse," said Sam. "It must be at the Big Foot Ranch. Take the pinto. She's a good horse. Bring 'er back to the Bar-X when you can."

"Bear, I'll take Brad and some men to get the gold,"

said the sheriff. "Adjust your saddle, and then you and Audrey can meet us at the cabin."

Sheriff Tate took Brad, some of the posse, and left for the cabin.

"I was scared when the posse stopped Ebony," said Audrey to Running Bear. "The message on the saddle said that you had been caught. It didn't say anything about Brad."

"Brad and I were scared, too. We did what we believed was correct at the time. Now we know it was the right thing to do."

"What do you mean, Bear?"

"I led them away from Brad and let them capture me. That gave Brad the opportunity to send for help, which he wisely did. You went to Riverton to bring the sheriff and a posse to the mine. Brad is a wise young man and you are an intelligent young lady. You are fortunate to have each other. I am pleased to have you as my friends."

"I never thought of it that way, Bear. I see what you mean."

"The saddle is adjusted. It is time to go join the posse at the cabin."

Running Bear and Audrey galloped out of the mine yard and took the road north toward the trail to the cabin.

It had been mid-afternoon when Sheriff Tate and his half of the posse left the Big Foot Mine. They saw a few deer and a black bear on the road north. Some of the men wished they were hunting game instead of robbers, but they obeyed Sheriff Tate's no shooting rule. The sheriff didn't want the robbers to know that someone else was in the area. The heat of the day was just starting to break as the posse reached the trail that led to the cabin.

Brad reined Ebony to a stop. When the posse had gathered around him, he said, "The cabin's on the trail, about two miles from here. I'll stop before we reach it so we can scout it out."

"Any questions, men?" asked the sheriff.

The men remained silent.

"Keep your rifles ready, and don't bunch up," said Harold Benton. "No need to be easy targets if they see us coming. It's single file from this point on."

Brad reined Ebony to the left and started up the trail. Sheriff Tate and rest of the posse followed, maintaining several lengths between each rider.

The posse had been riding for about ten minutes when Brad and the sheriff stopped and dismounted. The rest of the posse did the same and joined them.

"The cabin's about a hundred yards ahead," Brad said in a very soft voice. "It's just around the bend. It has one door in front and one small window on the side. It doesn't have a back door. There's one horse in front of the cabin. It may belong to one of the robbers."

"Sam, go to the right and get into a good position to cover us," directed the sheriff. "Signal me when you're ready. I'll take the rest of the men and cover the front door and the window."

Sheriff Tate deployed the men around the front and sides of the cabin. Sam waved at the sheriff, letting him know that he was ready. With the rest of the men in place, the sheriff dashed between boulders and trees until he was behind a large pine tree outside the cabin. The horse remained tethered in front of the cabin.

"You, in the cabin," he shouted. "This is Sheriff Tate of Riverton. I have a posse with me. Throw out your guns and come out with your hands up. I have the cabin surrounded." After shouting the warning, the sheriff quickly shielded himself behind the large tree.

The door slowly opened, followed by a rifle shot. The bullet knocked off a chunk of bark right where the sheriff's head had been. No order was needed. The men in the posse started shooting at the cabin.

After a few minutes, there was a pause in the fusillade. A man in the cabin shouted, "I give up! Stop the shooting!"

"Throw your guns out! Now!" commanded the sheriff.

The door opened wider and a rifle was thrown out, then a pistol.

"Keep your hands high, and come out slowly!"

The door opened and the gunman slowly came out with his hands raised over his head.

"Tell your partner to come out, too," said the sheriff.

"Partner?" questioned the man. "I'm the only one here."

"Sam. Take some men and check out the cabin," ordered the sheriff. "Don't take any chances. I don't want any members of my posse hurt."

While Sam and his men checked out the cabin, Sheriff Tate studied the man. He looked about 30 years old, medium build, and about five feet eight inches tall. The man's right boot was missing a metal toecap.

"No one's in the cabin," said Sam when he returned

to the sheriff. "There's only one horse, and that's it," he said, motioning to the bay tethered in front of the cabin.

Sam carefully removed the robber's gunbelt and then checked him for any hidden weapons.

Sheriff Tate looked the robber directly in the eye and said, "While Sam ties your hands, you can tell me your name and the names of your partners."

"Curly Pflug, and I don't have any partners," he replied innocently. "I'm passing through and was going to use the cabin for the night."

"I see that your right boot is missing a metal toecap. I have a toecap at my office that looks just like the one on your left boot. It was found where the stage was held up."

Curly showed surprise for a second, but quickly recovered and replied, "That don't mean nothin'; there's lotsa' boots with toecaps like mine."

"I'm sure that Zeke, Clay, and Slade will agree with you," replied the sheriff.

Again, Curly momentarily showed surprise at what Sheriff Tate had said. But before he could reply, the sheriff continued, "We've got to save Curly's partners from Big Foot. Sam, take him into town and lock him up. The Bentons will stay with me and get the gold for Big Foot. Even if they did rob the stage, we've got to save them from Big Foot."

"Big Foot!" exclaimed Curly. "There ain't no such thing as Big Foot."

"Tell that to Zeke, Clay, and Slade," said the sheriff.

"The sheriff's right," said Brad, "Big Foot's got Zeke, Clay, and Slade tied up inside the mine. He'll release them when I bring him the gold."

Curly looked questioningly at Brad, and then in a sneering voice said, "Kid, are you telling me you saw Big Foot?"

"That's right. Clay was helping me leave the mine when Big Foot grabbed us. Big Foot's big, really big. He's about seven feet tall and probably weighs three to four hundred pounds. And he stinks too; I mean he really stinks. His breath is so bad too it's worse than a pig pen on a hot summer day."

"That's enough, Brad," said the sheriff. "We've got to find the gold so we can free the men at the mine."

"Zeke gave me good directions," said Brad. "Let's go in the cabin and get the gold."

"The gold's in the cabin?" exclaimed Curly in disbelief.

Sherif Tate nodded toward Curly Pflug, "Sam, take your men and go lock him up, pronto!"

"You heard the sheriff," said Sam as he prodded Curly with his rifle. "Mount up. We have some riding to do."

♘

Jake Jackson, Sam, and their prisoner, Curly Pflug, followed the trail to the road north of the mine. The three men left the trail and started south on the road to Riverton when they saw Audrey and Running Bear coming toward them.

"You missed the shooting," yelled Jake. "This polecat was in the cabin and started shooting when the sheriff asked him to come out. When we started shooting back, he quickly saw the error of his way and obeyed the sheriff."

Running Bear nodded and then asked, "Did you see Big Foot?"

"No, maybe the shooting scared him away," said Jake.

Curly spoke up, "There ain't no such thing as Big Foot. It's just an old Injun legend."

"I thought Big Foot was just a legend too," replied Running Bear. "Then he captured me."

"I suppose he carried you under one arm," argued Curly.

"As a matter of fact, he did," replied Running Bear. "I gave an ancient Indian chant which offered him gold and silver for our lives. He agreed, so Zeke told Brad where to find the gold. Brad went to the cabin to get the gold."

"That's what the kid said, too," said Curly. "But I still don't believe there's such a thing as Big Foot."

"We've got to go," reminded Sam Burnes. "We're taking this polecat to the jail, Sheriff Tate's orders."

Brad, his father, and the sheriff entered the cabin. Brad went to the wood stove, looked at the rock floor underneath it and then knelt beside it. Reaching under the stove, he grasped the edge of a large flat stone and started wiggling it.

"Zeke said this stone would slide out," Brad explained. "The gold's supposed to be in the strongbox under the stone."

Harold Benton knelt on the other side of the stove and helped his son wiggle the stone. Together they pulled the large flat stone out from under the stove.

"Well I'll be," said the sheriff. "That's slicker'n

a greased pig at a county fair. It's there, just like Zeke said."

A well-dressed man carefully approached the cabin door. He wore a dark suit and vest. A gold watch chain ran from his belt to the pocket watch in his vest pocket. Raising his rifle, he quietly crept to the doorway of the cabin. He stood in the doorway for a moment and then said, "I'm glad Zeke gave good directions. If you want to go to this year's fair, raise your hands."

The man pointed a Henry rifle at the sheriff.

"No one needs to get hurt, it's best if you do exactly what I tell you to do."

"I'm not going to argue with a rifle," replied the sheriff. "What would you like us to do, Mister -- uh?"

"Just call me Clete, Clete Collins. You can begin by having the boy slowly push the strongbox to me."

Brad slowly pushed the box across the floor to Clete. "Zeke told me where the gold was so I could give it to Big Foot."

"Sorry to disappoint you, kid, but there is no Big Foot. Big Foot is just a legend, he doesn't exist."

"Yes, he does," insisted Brad. "He caught your friends called Zeke, Clay, Slade, and me in the mine and tied us up."

"I see. And just what does this Big Foot look like?"

"He's big, really big, Mr. Collins. He's about seven feet tall and weighs three to four hundred pounds," said Brad gesturing excitedly with his hands. "He stinks too, I mean really stinks. His breath is horrible, worse than a pig pen in the summer."

"And I suppose this Big Foot is outside waiting for the gold?"

"Yes, he's waiting for us in the forest. Big Foot followed us to get the gold. If we don't give him the gold, he'll eat Zeke, Clay, and Slade."

"Big Foot is just an Indian legend, kid. He doesn't exist."

Running Bear and Audrey followed the trail up the gentle slope to the cabin. The ride was pleasant as the trail was shaded from the afternoon sun by the tall trees. They rounded the bend in the trail and saw the clearing and front of the cabin.

"Stop," Running Bear whispered to Audrey.

"What is it?" asked Audrey softly as they turned their horses into a small grove of trees.

"A well-dressed man with a rifle is in front of the cabin," observed Running Bear.

"He must be one of the robbers; what can we do, Bear?"

"It is too late to shout a warning. We must do something else. I believe that Brad will tell him about Big Foot. We will try to scare him by throwing some large rocks at the cabin," said Running Bear.

"A sling can't throw a large rock that far," said Audrey. "We can't get closer without being seen, and that man has a rifle."

"We will use these young trees to help us. I will lift you up. Grab the top of this sapling and we will tie a rawhide thong to it."

Running Bear lifted Audrey so she could grasp the top of a young tree. He lowered her to the ground while she held the top of the tree with both hands. He quickly tied some rawhide thongs to the top of the tree and then tied the other end of one of the thongs to a large rock. He lifted Audrey again, and repeated the process with an adjacent small tree. Bear then tied the two rawhide thongs to a leather pouch with a rawhide loop.

"This looks like a large sling," said Audrey.

"You are very observant," replied Running Bear.

Running Bear then tied another rawhide strip around a large tree and tied a loop at the end of the rawhide. Together, they pulled the tops of the trees down with the loop on the leather pouch. The trees were held in the bowed position with a large stick stuck in the two rawhide loops.

"If we have built our sling properly, we should be able to hit the cabin with some large rocks," said Running Bear. "We have made a cannon without gunpowder."

"I see," said Audrey. "But Brad must convince the robber that the rocks are from Big Foot.

"Brad is an intelligent young man," said Running Bear. "We will find out. I will put a large rock in the pouch. Pull the stick when I say fire."

Running Bear placed a large rock in the leather pouch, and Audrey grasped the stick. Bear went to the side of the huge boulder and looked at the cabin.

"The man is still in the doorway. Fire," ordered Running Bear.

Audrey pulled the stick, the trees straightened up, and the rock hurtled toward the cabin.

The rock crashed into the side of the cabin. Clete Collins instinctively stepped inside the cabin and closed the door.

"It's Big Foot," yelled Brad. "He wants his gold."

"You've got the gold and the rifle," said the sheriff. "Take them and go. Just leave us our weapons so we can defend ourselves from Big Foot."

The horses whinnied, pulled themselves free of the hitching rail, and galloped away from the cabin.

"Must be a bear outside," said Clete. "Horses always spook when a bear's around."

"I suppose bears throw big rocks at cabins too," said Brad.

The cabin shook as another rock smashed into it. This rock hit the front door, knocking it wide open.

Clete Collin's eyes bulged out in fear as he stammered, "That can't be a bear. Bears don't throw rocks, and a man isn't strong enough to throw rocks that big. But Big Foot is only an Indian Legend. Big Foot doesn't exist."

"We thought the same thing," replied Harold Benton. "But the Big Foot legend tells about his strength."

"He's big and strong," added Brad. "He picked Zeke up and carried him under one arm."

"Well," declared Clete, "I'll just go outside and see how Big Foot likes hot lead. Kid, bring me those six-shooters and rifles."

Brad followed the instructions and brought the sheriff's and his father's pistols to Clete. Clete watched very carefully as Brad picked up the rifles by their barrels and laid them by the strongbox.

"Kid, since you know this Big Foot, tell him I'm coming out with the gold," said Clete.

Brad edged along the wall to the door of the cabin and shouted, "Big Foot, don't throw any more rocks. I'm bringing the gold out."

Audrey looked at Running Bear and asked, "How do you say 'okay' in Big Foot language?"

Running Bear turned both of his hands palms up and said, "I'll try hawoop, hawoop."

Cupping his hands around his mouth, Running Bear made a couple of deep guttural sounds, "Hawoop! Hawoop!"

Brad looked at Mr. Collins and said, "I think that means okay. Shall I take the strongbox out?"

"You do that," said Clete. "Take it about 30 feet straight out the front door. Put the rifles and six-shooters beside it. Then come back in here with your friends. I'll take care of this Big Foot when he comes down for the gold."

Brad pulled the strongbox out of the cabin and left it an open area as Clete had directed. Under Clete's watchful eyes, he returned to the cabin and brought out the two pistols, placing them beside the strongbox. Then he did the same with the two rifles.

"Audrey. Let's get another rock ready. The two pistols and two rifles are from your father and the sheriff. The robber still has his pistol and rifle."

The young trees were bent down again and another rock was placed for release. Audrey grasped the stick that would release the rawhide thongs and send the rock hurtling toward the cabin. Running Bear went to the side of the boulder and looked at the cabin.

"Brad is in the cabin. Fire!" said Running Bear.

Audrey pulled the stick, and the young trees threw the rock toward the cabin. Brad and the three men flinched when the rock struck the roof.

"We put out the gold and the guns. Why did he throw another rock?" asked Clete.

"Big Foot's smart," replied Brad. "He saw Sheriff Tate and my father enter the cabin with their weapons. Then he saw you enter with your rifle and pistol. That makes three rifles and three pistols. I only took out two rifles and two pistols."

"We're goin'a do things my way now," snarled Clete angrily. "Kid, get that rope. Tie up the sheriff and your old man. Tie them to those bunks, and be quick."

"Yes, sir," said Brad. Brad's father and Sheriff Tate quickly went to the bunks. Brad tied them to the bunk under Clete's watchful eyes.

"That's a pretty good job of tying, kid. Now I'll tie you to the bunk."

Brad sat on the floor as Clete tied Brad's hands together on the pole supporting the top bunk. Clete stood up and looked at Brad, then at Sheriff Tate and Harold Benton.

"I'm pretty good with the rope, too," said Clete. "Now I'll go take care of this Big Foot. But first, I need another pistol. This rusty ol' pistol I found under the bunk is goin' to help."

Clete placed his good pistol in his boot. Then he opened the cabin door and slowly walked out to the strongbox with his rifle and the rusty pistol. He placed his rifle with the other two rifles and the rusty pistol with the other pistols.

"Big Foot," shouted Clete. "Here's the gold and the weapons. Come on down! How about I give you three people for some of the gold?"

"He's too confident," said Running Bear. "He probably has a back-up pistol. We'll send another rock."

"This rock is bigger than the last one. Shall I use it?"

"Yes," said Running Bear. "It will fall short of the cabin, but it may cause him to throw out his back-up pistol. Fire it when I start hawooping."

Big Foot cupped his hands and yelled, "Hawoop! Hawoop! Hawooooooop!"

Audrey pulled the stick from the loops and the two young trees hurled another rock toward the cabin.

CHAPTER 7
BIG FOOT DISARMS A ROBBER

Inside the cabin, the top bunk creaked as Brad pushed it up and slipped the rope off the post. He was cutting the rope from his father's hands when he heard Running Bear's hawoops.

Clete heard the creaking and turned his head to see what was causing the creaking sound. Clete had no way of knowing that Audrey had just released another rock. Since this rock was slightly larger than the earlier rocks, it fell Short of the cabin and struck Clete in the abdomen, knocking the wind out of him. He staggered, clasped his midsection, and fell to the ground, his mouth opening and closing like a fish out of water as he tried to fill his lungs with air.

Brad heard the hawooping and said, "Running Bear's up to something, Pa. Untie your feet while I free Sheriff Tate. Maybe we can escape."

Brad and his father heard Big Foot hawooping, but couldn't see Clete. Sheriff Tate, however, had a clear view of Clete in front of the cabin and saw him fall to the ground.

"Maybe we can just walk outside, pick up our weapons, and take Clete to jail," said the sheriff. "He's flopping around on the ground like a fish out of water."

Harold Benton pulled the ropes from his feet and ran out the door. He picked up his rifle and holstered his pistol while keeping an eye on Clete. When Clete started to sit up, Harold poked him in the back with the rifle barrel.

"I think Big Foot would like to see you carefully pull that pistol from your boot and throw it next to the strongbox."

Clete's eyes were wide open with terror, and his face contorted in pain. He nodded his head weakly and pulled the pistol from his boot. Gasping in little breaths of air, he meekly threw his pistol toward the strongbox.

"Maybe we can save you from Big Foot," said the sheriff. "I don't think he'll attack two armed men. We'll also try to save your partners back at the mine."

"I don't know what Big Foot did to you," said Harold Benton, "but we'd better get moving. Can you stand up?"

"I'll try to get up," gasped Clete. "He hit me in the stomach. Big Foot hit me in the stomach, but I never saw him."

"Here come Audrey and Running Bear," said Brad. "Maybe they saw Big Foot."

"Running Bear, did you see Big Foot?" asked the sheriff.

"No, but we heard him hawooping. He must have heard us coming and hid. Right now, he's probably in the forest watching us."

Audrey looked at Clete and said, "Sheriff Tate, you haven't introduced me to the new member of your posse."

"Well, he's not a member of the posse. He came to meet his partners and collect his share of the gold from the robbery. We told him that Big Foot wanted the gold to free his partners, but he had other plans. Seems he wanted to keep the gold, cheat or bushwhack Big Foot, and abandon his partners. He didn't say what plans he had for us."

Audrey looked at Clete with a shocked expression and exclaimed, "You're mean! You'd leave your partners with Big Foot? That's horrible! You'd let your own partners be eaten by Big Foot?"

Running Bear kept a solemn face as he watched Audrey turn away from Clete. She buried her face in her father's chest to stifle her laughter.

"Big Foot spooked the horses. I'll get them," said Brad. "Three of the horses are close by."

"We've got to ride fast to beat Big Foot back to the mine to save his partners," said the sheriff. "Running Bear, tie this outlaw to his horse. I don't want him getting loose."

Running Bear began tying Clete's hands together. By the time he had finished tying them, Brad arrived with Clete's horse.

"Mount up Clete, and remember that I have a rifle," said Harold Benton.

When he was mounted, Bear tied Clete's hands to the saddle's pommel.

"Good job, Bear. Take his rifle and guard him while we take care of the strongbox," said the sheriff.

Harold Benton and the sheriff tied the strongbox behind the Audrey's saddle. Running Bear continued guarding Clete as the others mounted their horses.

"Here's your horse," said Brad as he handed the pinto's reins to Running Bear.

"Harold," said Sheriff Tate, "you take the lead with

Brad and Audrey. Audrey, since you weigh the least, the strongbox is on your horse." The sheriff looked at Running Bear and continued, "Bear, I'll fall in behind the Bentons, then Clete. You take the rear. I want Clete between us."

Hank Lacy and Sam Burns took a couple of lanterns and went into the mine. In a few minutes they reached the enlarged area with the crates.

"Anybody here?" shouted Hank.

"Help!" yelled Zeke. "We're back here."

"Keep talking. We'll follow your voice," replied Hank.

Hank and Sam followed Zeke's shouting. In a few minutes they found Zeke, Clay, and Slade in the small side shaft with the air vent.

"Quick. Untie me," pleaded Zeke.

"Who tied you up?" asked Sam.

"Big Foot!" exclaimed Zeke. "Please untie us so we can leave before he comes back and eats us."

"Big Foot is an old Indian legend. There isn't a Big Foot," said Hank.

"We're looking for a kid named Brad. Have you seen him?" asked Sam.

"Yes! He's getting the gold to give to Big Foot," explained Zeke.

"Gold?" said Hank questioningly.

"Yes! Gold to give to Big Foot for our freedom," said Zeke. "Please, you gotta' untie us."

"Where's this kid going to get the gold?" asked Hank.

"At the cabin where we hid it," said Zeke.

"Why would you hide gold in a cabin when you can put it in the bank?" asked Sam.

"Please, just untie us," begged Zeke.

"We'd better go," said Hank. "I don't want to anger whoever hog-tied these chaps."

"You're right," said Sam. "Some outlaws might have tied 'em up. Maybe it was a lawman that tied em' up. If we untied them, we could get in a heap of trouble."

"No! Don't go!" pleaded Zeke. "Please untie us. Don't let Big Foot eat us."

"Tell us about this gold, and I'll think about cutting some ropes," said Sam.

"It's the gold from the Overland Stage! Now, untie us."

"You're the ones that robbed the stage?" asked Hank.

"Yes. Please untie us. Don't let Big Foot eat us."

"Since you admit to robbing the stage, we'll have to take you to the sheriff in Riverton. Is that what you want, or would you rather stay here?" asked Sam.

"Take us to the sheriff, take us anywhere, but please don't leave us here for Big Foot," pleaded Zeke.

"That's right," begged Slade. "Get us out of here."

"We'd rather go to jail than be Big Foot food," begged Clay. "Please untie us."

"Since they admitted to robbing the stage, we have to take them in," said Hank. "Untie their feet, and we'll put them on the horses at the mine office."

Sam cut the ropes that tied their feet together and helped them stand up. Hank kept them covered them with his pistol.

"Now head for the entrance," ordered Hank. "Sam, hold the lantern high so they can see."

The five men slowly moved to the entrance of the

mine. In a few minutes the light at the entrance could be seen.

"There's the mine entrance!" exclaimed Slade as he bumped into the side of the mineshaft.

"And some deputies are outside waiting for us," said Hank.

"Unless Big Foot got them," added Sam.

"Dooley, help these varmints onto their horses," said Hank. "We're taking them to the Riverton Jail."

"They robbed the Overland Stage," explained Sam Burns. "Don't take any chances."

"Did you find the Brad Benton?" asked Dooley.

"They said the he went to a cabin to get the Overland gold for Big Foot," answered Hank.

"I thought Big Foot was just an Indian legend," said Dooley.

"He ain't no legend!" exclaimed Zeke. "He conked me, Slade, and Clay. Running Bear talked Big Foot into freein' us for the gold. Running Bear and the kid are getting the gold for Big Foot now."

"We'd better get going before Big Foot returns," said Dooley.

"Sam, pick two men and take the lead," said Hank Lacy. "I'll take the rear with the rest of the men. We'll put Big Foot's dinner between us."

"Like the meat in a sandwich," said Dooley.

"That's right," said Sam. "Like the meat in a Big Foot sandwich."

"Move 'em out," said Hank. "And keep a lookout for Big Foot. I don't want Big Foot to dine on Bar-X men."

Hank stopped the posse at the sheriff's office. The Bar-X hands didn't need to be told what to do. They quickly dismounted, yanked the outlaws off their horses, and shoved them into the sheriff's office.

"I've got the keys," declared Hank. "If they're in the jail, they should be safe from Big Foot."

The jail was made of stone with square iron bars set in the stone walls. Each cell had two bunks, a bucket, and a small window six feet above the floor. The bunks were three feet wide and six feet long. In addition, each bunk had a blanket and a thin pillow. Zeke and Clay were placed in a cell on the north side of the jail. Slade was placed alone in a cell on the south side of the jail.

"Slade, I hope Brad and that Indian find the gold. If they don't, I just might take you back to the mine," threatened Hank.

"You can't do that," wailed Slade. "We're in jail. You have to protect us."

"I'm not the sheriff," said Hank. "Besides, we just might take you back to the mine to gather some evidence. Isn't that right, boys?"

"Whatever you say," agreed Dooley.

"Once we get there, you just might escape. You'd escape hog-tied, of course, inside Big Foot's cave," predicted Hank.

Zeke, Clay and Slade exchanged fearful looks as the Bar-X hands laughed.

Jake Jackson stopped his small posse in front of the sheriff's office and dismounted. Hank Lacy and the Bar-X men came out to see who had arrived.

"The sheriff's office has a nice cell for you," said Jake. "I'm sure you'll like your accommodations. It looks like your partners are already here."

Curly looked at the sheriff's office and thought about what lay ahead. There'd be a trial. He'd probably go to prison. He remembered his first meeting with Clete Collins. Clete had made the robbery sound so easy. No one would get hurt. The five of them would split the gold. Then every four to six months, they'd put on their Big Foot costume and commit another robbery. They'd even leave some footprints from Big Foot when they committed a robbery to scare folks. Big Foot would be blamed for the robberies.

"Git down, you polecat," barked Jake. "Thieves go to jail, and that's where you're goin'."

Curly dismounted and walked up the steps to the sheriff's office. He saw a man standing in the doorway with a deputy's badge pinned to his shirt.

"Welcome to Riverton's finest jail," greeted Hank Lacy with a smile. "Please go straight ahead. Your cell is the second door on the right. You'll be bunking with a fellow member of your gang."

The cell door was opened and Curly entered Slade's cell. Once Curly was inside, Hank re-locked the cell door.

"Put your hands through the bars, and I'll untie those ropes," offered Hank. "We'll keep the ropes, just in case we have to take you back to the mine. I might need your help in finding some clues. I might even trade you to Big Foot."

"There ain't no such thing as Big Foot," grumbled Curly. "That's just an old Injun legend."

"You're wrong," declared Zeke. "There is a Big Foot. He hit me and tied me up."

"That's right," confirmed Clay. "He conked and tied me up too. We'd be Big Foot's dinner if'n Brad and that Injun hadn't saved us."

"I thought that Big Foot was just a legend too," added Slade. "That Injun was hog-tied with the rest of us at the mine. Then he did some Injun chant to Big Foot, and that critter came and yanked him up. That Injun talked to Big Foot, used sign language, or somethin'. He got that crazy critter to agree to swap us for the gold. Then, Mr. Lacy was with a search party out looking for that kid named Brad and found us. He wouldn't untie us till we told him who tied us up. He was afraid of making someone mad. We had to tell him the whole story, or he'd a left us in the mine for Big Foot."

"There ain't no Big Foot," insisted Curly. "That's just an old Injun legend."

"Mr. Lacy thought that Big Foot was just a legend too," added Zeke. "But I know better. I saw what he can do. There ain't no man that can capture three armed men and tie 'em up. There is a Big Foot. Just ask that kid."

"Maybe you're right," conceded Curly. "The kid said Big Foot was really big, about seven feet tall and weighed 300 to 400 pounds. He also said the critter stunk and that he smelled worse than a pig pen on a hot summer day."

"I hope Sheriff Tate doesn't get caught by Big Foot," said Hank Lacy. "If the sheriff doesn't get back by sundown, we're taking the four of you back to the mine.

I'm sure Big Foot will take four men in exchange for one sheriff."

"You can't do that," protested Slade. "You're the law. You have to protect us."

"As I said before," replied Hank, "We'll take you along to help us find the sheriff. We can't help it if you just happen to escape while we're searching for the sheriff."

"And maybe Big Foot will be real nice and give us the sheriff," laughed Sam Burnes.

Sheriff Tate stopped his small posse at the entrance to the Big Foot Mine. "We'll rest here for a few minutes," he said. "Running Bear, take Brad with you and let Big Foot know that we have the gold."

Running Bear and Brad dismounted and entered the mine. They walked about twenty feet and stopped.

"We'll wait here a few minutes," whispered Running Bear.

"Then we'll come out and exclaim that they're gone," replied Brad softly.

"That is correct," agreed Running Bear.

Clete fidgeted in his saddle and stared at the mine entrance. Sheriff Tate talked about the deer grazing on the side of the hill while he watched Clete out of the corner of his eyes.

Clete finally broke his silence. "Sheriff, we'll have to ride double. We don't have horses for Slade, Clay and Zeke."

"Don't worry about that. I'm sure they'd rather walk than be a dinner for Big Foot."

Audrey pointed to a large buck on the ridge behind the mine. "He seems to be watching us."

"He probably is," replied her father. "One watches while the others graze.

"What's taking them so long?" grumbled Clete Collins. "All they have to do is untie their feet and bring them out."

"Running Bear is probably talking to Big Foot," replied Audrey.

"Here they come," said Harold Benton.

Running Bear and Brad exited the mine and stopped in front of Sheriff Tate.

"They're not there!" exclaimed Brad. "Slade, Clay, and Zeke are gone!"

"Big Foot must have taken them to another cave when he didn't get the gold. He is probably watching us right at this moment," concluded Running Bear.

"We'd better leave now," said the sheriff. "It looks like they're going to be food for Big Foot."

"You can't just leave them!" shouted Clete. "You have to find them!"

"There is nothing that we can do," said Running Bear. "Big Foot is angry because you tried to trick him at the cabin. We must leave now, before Big Foot comes after us."

"Same as before," directed the sheriff, "Harold, Audrey and Brad in front. Running Bear and I'll take the rear with Clete."

Harold gently urged his horse to a trot. Brad and Audrey did the same and came abreast of their father. Clete looked around nervously as he fell in behind the Bentons.

The sun was low in the sky as Sheriff Tate and his small posse rode down the street with Clete Collins tied to his horse. Some members of the posse had already gone home and told their wives about the Big Foot Gang. Their wives had told their friends, friends had told their friends, and soon most of Riverton knew about the gang. Citizens of Riverton who had come out to watch for them shouted, "Good job, Sheriff. We're behind you all the way," and made other supportive comments as he rode to the jail with Clete.

The small posse stopped in front of the sheriff's office and dismounted. Clete remained on his horse, his hands tied to the saddle's pommel.

"Good news travels fast," observed Harold Benton. "The rest of your posse must have already arrived."

"That's where you'll be staying for the next week, Clete," said Sheriff Tate. "You'll be sharing the jail with your partner, Curly Pflug."

"First, I'll put Clete in jail with his friend Curly," said the sheriff. "Then, I think I'll go to the barber shop for a bath. Miss Jones and I are having dinner at the Riverton Hotel tonight. What about you folks?"

"I'm going home for one of Victoria's dinners and then to bed," replied Harold. "We've got church tomorrow, and Abby's got a new hymn to teach us tonight. Running Bear, you're invited to join us for dinner and stay the night. Abby and Victoria haven't seen you for some time. Will you join us?"

"Please say yes," requested Audrey.

Running Bear smiled and said, "Yes, I would like very much to join your family for dinner. I cannot say no to one of Victoria's meals, and Gentle Water does not expect me home until Sunday evening."

"Sheriff Tate," offered Brad. "Audrey and I'll take your horse to the livery."

"I'd appreciate that, Brad. And please take Clete's horse too." Turning to Harold and Bear, he continued. "Bring in the strongbox while I take this varmint to join his partner. I'm sure he'd like to hear how Clete angered Big Foot, causing Zeke, Clay, and Slade to remain Big Foot's captives."

"It will be a pleasure," said Running Bear.

"Brad, Audrey," said their father. "We'll meet at my office and ride home together."

"Okay. We want to see Ma's face when the four of us ride up," said Brad.

Brad and Audrey took the two horses to the livery and arranged for their grooming and some oats. As they were leaving the livery, Audrey asked, "Weren't you scared at the mine?"

"Of course I was. But I was too busy helping to free Running Bear to know it. He risked his life to protect me. I had to try to rescue him. I couldn't live with myself if I hadn't at least tried."

"I'm glad that you succeeded and that you weren't hurt."

"Do you think Pa'll get Mr. Goldman to open the bank today?" asked Brad. "He doesn't want to leave the gold in the sheriff's office overnight."

"Knowing Pa, I'm sure he'll convince old man Goldman to open the bank. The fact that today is Saturday only makes it a bigger challenge for Pa. He'll succeed."

"You're right again," agreed Brad. "I see Pa coming

out of the bank now with Running Bear and old man Goldman."

Brad and Audrey entered the sheriff's office. Sheriff Tate, Hank Lacy, and some of the Bar-X men greeted them.

"What was it like to talk to Big Foot?" asked Hank.

"It was terrible," replied Brad. "He was furry, he stinks, and his breath was horrible. I never want to see, or smell him, again."

"You may have to," said Sam, "The judge might need Big Foot to testify at the trial."

"We could take the gang back to the mine to find additional evidence," suggested Hank. "Maybe we'll see Big Foot while we're there."

"Not the mine," shouted Clay. "Big Foot's there. He might capture us again."

"I'll testify," offered Brad. "I saw everything that Big Foot saw."

"There's a reward for the capture of the robbers," said Sheriff Tate. "Have you thought about what you'll do with the money?"

"Running Bear gets half," stated Audrey.

"That's right," confirmed Brad. "He helped us, and he taught us how to track the robbers. We agreed to give him half of the reward if we found the robbers. He'll use the reward to get new books and desks for his school."

"He'll be able to buy a lot of books with a thousand dollars," said Hank. "Especially since we'll be helping him build some desks and fix up the school."

"That's a thank you from the Bar-X," confirmed

Sam. "With the Big Foot gang behind bars, our cattle will stop disappearing."

"You two better get over to the stage office," said the sheriff. "Your father and Running Bear are probably there waiting for you. Besides, you don't want to make Running Bear late for dinner with Victoria."

Victoria stopped briefly at the front door and looked at the road. "Abby, I see four riders coming this way. I think two of them are Brad and Audrey."

Abby got up from the piano, where she had been practicing the new hymn, and joined her mother on the front porch. "Yes, that's Brad, Audrey, Harold, and the fourth rider is--," Abby paused while she tried to identify the fourth rider, "It's Running Bear!" she exclaimed. "We haven't seen Running Bear for a year!"

Audrey and her father were riding beside each other on the trail to their barn. "Pa," said Audrey, "Ma and Nana are on the porch. I'll bet they're surprised to see Running Bear."

"I'm sure they are. I believe it was about a year ago that you visited us. Is that right, Bear?"

"Yes, that is right. Victoria had baked her famous apple-blackberry pie. I remember it very well."

The foursome rode directly to the barn and dismounted. Abby and Victoria hitched up their skirts and rushed to the barn. "Welcome back, Bear," greeted Victoria. "And before you ask, the answer is yes. I have baked an apple-blackberry pie."

"Audrey!" exclaimed Abby as she saw the bloody

bandage on her daughter's arm. "What in the world happened to you?"

"It's just a cut, Ma, nothing exciting."

"Nothing exciting!" exclaimed her father. "You led Sheriff Tate and the posse to the stagecoach robbers. You call that nothing?"

Abby's mouth opened in amazement at her husband's revelation. She faced her daughter and asked, "You led a posse to the stagecoach robbers? How can you call that nothing?"

"Well it's nothing compared to what Brad did," Audrey replied with a big smile as she nodded toward her brother. "He conked a robber on the head and rescued Running Bear."

Abby and Victoria looked at Brad in disbelief. They tried to comprehend what Audrey had just told them.

"Well, I had to, Ma. Running Bear let them capture him so that I wouldn't get caught. He risked his life for me."

Choking up, but maintaining her composure, Abby softly said, "Bear thank you for taking care my children. I don't know how to repay you for letting them capture you so my son could remain free."

"I have already been repaid," replied Running Bear. "You son risked his freedom to rescue me."

"This is too much to talk about out here!" exclaimed Victoria. "Take care of those horses, wash up, and you can tell us the whole story at dinner. Come along, Abby. We've got to get dinner on the table."

Victoria started back to the house. Abby's eyes were starting to tear as Victoria took her arm and pulled her toward the house.

Brad hooked the stirrup over the saddle and began un-cinching Blaze's saddle. Audrey watched her brother's thoughtful act and said, "I'll get the oats."

Harold and Running Bear began unsaddling their horses. By the time they finished, Audrey had arrived with four feed bags, each with a scoop of oats.

"I see you've been listening to Nana's words of wisdom," said Brad as he tried to hide a smile. He turned his back to Audrey as he began to remove Ebony's saddle. "The quickest way to a horse's heart is through its stomach."

"I've never heard her say anything like that, Brad. When did she talk about oats for horses?"

Running Bear smiled and explained, "I believe Victoria said that the quickest way to a man's heart is through his stomach."

Harold Benton stifled his laughter as he looked at his daughter's puzzled face. As Audrey realized the twisted meaning of Brad's quotation her face expressed shock and then it turned red. She was embarrassed that she had fallen for her own kind of word trap, yet she was impressed that her brother had been able to trap her with such a misquote.

"Brad Benton!" she exclaimed, "You--! You--! You're terrible! You really got me with that one."

Harold Benton laughed at his children and then said, "Now that the horses have been fed, we'd better wash up and get some of your grandmother's cooking. Your grandmother is going to want a detailed account of what happened today. And I need answers to a number of questions. Overland Stage will want a report about how you tracked and captured the robbers."

The four washed the dirt and sweat off their hands and faces. Abby had thoughtfully placed a couple of towels by the pump earlier that afternoon. They dried themselves and headed for the house. Brad opened the front door for Running Bear and his father.

"I thought a long time before I came up with that one," said Brad as Audrey entered the house.

"You really suckered me. I fell for it hook, line, and sinker. It was a good one. Let's eat."

Abby and her mother had prepared a marvelous meal. Roast venison, string beans, Abby's fresh biscuits, fresh carrots from the root cellar, and baked potatoes. Abby, Audrey, and Brad had lemonade as usual. Running Bear, Harold, and Victoria had coffee.

Harold blessed the meal and added a short prayer thanking the Lord for protecting them through their venturesome day.

"Bear, why did you help Brad and Audrey look for the robbers' trail?" asked Victoria.

"I supervised their tracking. One could call it a final exam for what I taught them last summer. And, my school needs new books. Half of the two-thousand-dollar reward will buy many books," said Running Bear as he looked at Brad and Audrey.

"Half of two thousand dollars?" questioned Abby as she cut a piece of venison.

"Yes, Brad and Audrey told me about the two-thousand-dollar reward."

"We told him about the reward and asked him to help us," explained Audrey. "He said his school needed new books. We needed his tracking skills to find the robber's trail. So we agreed that we'd split the reward."

120

"It gets even better," added Harold Benton putting down a biscuit. "Hank Lacy and his men from the Bar-X are going to repair the school for free. They believe that their cattle will stop disappearing now that the Big Foot Gang is behind bars."

"I thought you captured the stagecoach robbers, not rustlers," questioned Abby.

"We did. But the robbers are from the Big Foot Ranch, which is next to the Bar-X. The Bar-X has been losing cattle over the years. They suspected the men at the Big Foot Ranch, but had no proof. Now with the foreman and his hands behind bars, the owner will probably sell the ranch. The Big Foot Ranch is too small to be a profitable ranch, but it would make a nice addition to the Bar-X. Aaron Wellman, who owns the Bar-X, has offered several times to buy the Big Foot. Maybe he'll get it this time."

Abby looked quizzically at her husband, and then posed a question. "Since Brad and Audrey are your children, will Overland allow them to receive the reward?"

"They put no restrictions on the reward. And Sheriff Tate had not been able to track the robbers. I don't think they'll be hesitant about the reward."

Brad finished a bite of venison and added, "Especially when you tell them about the Big Foot costume."

"Big Foot costume?" questioned their mother.

"Yes," explained Running Bear. "The gang had a costume that resembled Big Foot. They were going to do more robberies and blame Big Foot for them."

Abby paused with her glass of lemonade halfway to her lips and said, "But Big Foot is just a legend. There really isn't a Big Foot, is there?"

"Indian legends describe Big Foot," said Running Bear. "In 1864, the *Statesman,* an Idaho newspaper, reported that a fur trader was attacked by some hairy creatures. They called these hairy creatures Big Foot.

In the 1840s, Reverend Walker had a mission north of Spokane, Washington. The Indians told him about a race of hairy giants that lived in the mountains. Again, Big Foot," explained Running Bear.

"Where did you hear those stories?" asked Harold.

"At the college," replied Running Bear. "I read the back copies of the newspapers."

"You did spend a lot of time in the library reading," said Abby. "Now I know what you read in those newspapers."

"Then there really is a Big Foot," said Brad in amazement. "You told me it was just an Indian legend."

"It is an Indian legend," replied Running Bear. "I did not say it was true and I did not say it was false."

Brad looked hopefully at Running Bear, and then continued. "But what about that newspaper story in Idaho? And the hairy giant the reverend at the mission school talked about? There must be truth in those stories about Big Foot."

"Newspaper editors sometimes print what will sell newspapers. They do not always wish to print just the truth. What is important is that the robbers believe in Big Foot. They are not Christians; they do not believe in God. But now, they believe in Big Foot. They have confessed because they fear Big Foot. Mr. Lacy and I told them we will take them back to Big Foot's mine if they do not tell the truth about the stage robbery."

Victoria slowly set down her cup of coffee. Running Bear's statement about the robbers left her momentarily stunned. Then her face broke out in a big smile and she exclaimed, "You made them believe in Big Foot!"

"That is true. But I also had the help of two young actors," replied Running Bear. "Brad and Audrey also said they saw Big Foot."

Looking at her children, Abby Benton said, "You didn't." She paused for a moment, put her fingers to her mouth and continued, "You did! You told them that you saw Big Foot!"

"It helped us escape and capture the robbers," explained Brad. "Besides, it was Running Bear's chant that really made them believe in Big Foot."

"Audrey is a good actress too," added her father. "She told Clete Collins that he was a horrible man because he was willing to let his partners be eaten by Big Foot. Of course, she had to bury her face in my chest to hide her laughter."

Abby looked out the window and said, "They could spend the rest of their lives believing in Big Foot."

Victoria stood up and said, "That's enough about Big Foot; let's clear the table. Then, we can sing the new hymn a few times before we turn in."

Brad and Audrey took the dirty dishes to the kitchen. Victoria put the leftover roast in the icebox while Brad and Audrey washed and dried the dishes. Abby practiced the new hymn while Running Bear and Harold refilled the woodbox in the kitchen. After the chores were completed, they all went to the living room.

"Gather behind me and we'll sing the new hymn," said Abby. "'God of Our Fathers' has been declared the National Hymn of the United States."

As the family sang the unfamiliar words for the first

time, Audrey reflected on their meaning in light of the day's events. "Ma," she said, "the second verse seems to describe how we were guided today. It begins, 'Thy love divine, hath led us in the past. In this free land by Thee our lot is cast.'"

"Hymns are songs of praise to the Lord," replied her mother. "I'm pleased that you found a personal meaning to the words. When you sing the hymn tomorrow, you'll be thanking the Lord for helping to capture the robbers."

The family sang the hymn several times before they felt comfortable with it. "That does it," announced their mother.

"I'm going to turn in," said Brad. "It's been a long day, and I'm really tired. How about you, Audrey?"

"Tonight, I'll probably fall asleep before you do."

"Bear, do you remember where the guestroom is?" asked Victoria.

"Yes. It is the room where the morning sun helps me begin the day."

"You are so poetic," said Abby. "But, you always were very descriptive."

"I'm bushed, and tomorrow will be here before we know it. I'll see you all in the morning," said Harold as he climbed the stairs to the bedroom.

CHAPTER 8
SUNDAY MORNING

"Looks like it's going to be a full church today, Reverend," said Jake Jackson.

"Bless the Lord," said Reverend Wesley.

"Ya' better bless Brad, Audrey, and Running Bear too," replied Jake. "They did the trackin' and capturin'. The posse just brought 'em in."

The Riverton Community Church had a record attendance on Sunday, May 30, 1880. The posse had told their spouses and friends about capturing the Big Foot Gang. The spouses and friends, of course, had told their friends. With each retelling, the Big Foot Gang got bigger and meaner and the deeds of Brad, Audrey, and Running Bear grew to heroic proportions. Since Abby Benton was pianist at the church, folks just naturally knew that Brad, Audrey and their father would be singing Sunday morning when Abby played the piano. By attending church, folks figured they'd be able to see Riverton's newest heroine and heroes.

The Bentons and Running Bear received many thanks from friends as they arrived at church. Reverend Rob Wesley even mentioned the capture of the gang in his sermon and praised the bravery of Brad, Audrey, and Running Bear for helping to put the gang behind bars.

After the service, Brad moved down the aisle with Audrey and Running Bear. The congregation was congratulating Reverend Wesley on his sermon. Some friends of Brad and Audrey, however, wanted to see them first.

"Brad, congratulations on capturing the gang," said Buck Hodges as he gave his friend a pat on the back.

"I couldn't have done it without Audrey and Running Bear," said Brad. "We worked together to find the robbers. Running Bear even risked his life for me."

"Brad also risked his life for me," added Running Bear as he put his hand on Brad's shoulder. "That is all we can say until after the trial."

"When's the trial?" asked Buck.

Brad turned to his father and said, "Pa, have you heard when the trial's going to be held?"

"Judge Callahan will probably have it next week. He likes swift justice." Harold turned to David P. Acker, owner of the Riverton Hotel, and asked, "When do you think the trial will be, David?"

David smiled and said, "I've already reserved the dining room for the judge. The trial will start at nine o'clock Friday morning. We'll set up some tables in the lobby for those folks that might want a late breakfast. I've even reserved two rooms for the Overland Stage folks, just in case they send someone to the trial. Hope you don't object."

"No objection from me, thanks for thinking of them."

"Tell your Ma I liked the new hymn, 'God of Our Fathers,' said Wilma Sue as she kissed Audrey on the cheek.

"I'll do that," replied Audrey.

Sheriff Tate moved through the pews to the Bentons and said, "Congressman Garfield's train will be arriving Tuesday at nine o'clock. I got the telegram just as I was leaving to come to church. Can I count on you men to be some of my deputies that morning?"

"Sure," replied Harold.

"You can count on me too," added David Acker.

"It will be an honor to be your deputy," said Running Bear.

"I knew I could count on you folks," said the sheriff, "Tuesday, my office at half past seven. I'll assign duties at that time."

"Pa!" exclaimed Audrey, "you'll be a deputy again."

"Yes, I'll be a deputy again. It's part of being a good citizen. Just as we give money to the church to help others, citizens must give to the government to help others. Our taxes pay Sheriff Tate, but sometimes taxes aren't enough. He needed help to capture the Big Foot Gang, so some of Riverton's men volunteered to help. He needs help again on Tuesday when Congressman Garfield comes to Riverton. I'm giving some of my time that morning to help, same as some other men will be doing."

"I never thought of it that way," said Brad. "It's a voluntary tax, kind of like a tithe to Riverton."

"Yes, just like the men from the Bar-X repairing our school next week," added Running Bear. "These voluntary contributions are what make a democracy strong. The Bible says to help thy neighbor. Helping others is part of being a good citizen."

"Bear, you sound like a preacher," said Reverend Wesley. "And please remember that the church is available for your use when you bring your students to Riverton."

"I cannot forget. My students keep asking when we will visit Riverton again."

"Pa," said Brad. "Audrey and I'll be in the balcony helping Betty Jones and Angus McTavish review their school work."

"Fine, I'll come get you when we're ready to go home." Then he and Running Bear headed toward Hank Lacy and the Bar-X men under a big tree.

"Thank you for bringing my horse with you, Mr. Lacy," said Running Bear. "I also thank you for the loan of your pinto."

"We must thank you, Bear," replied Hank. "Our cattle should stop disappearing now that the Big Foot Gang is in jail. How about a school fixing barbecue next Saturday? We'll bring the steer, tools, and lumber."

"That would be very nice," said Running Bear. "My wife will talk to the other squaws and we will have a big barbecue."

"Bear, you better stop by for Sunday dinner," said Harold Benton. "Victoria said she can't let you return on an empty stomach."

The families of Riverton met in small groups under the trees that were around the church. Since church was a major social event of the week, it provided the opportunity to meet friends and hear what was happening. Some families even brought tables and had a Sunday picnic behind the church. There was a lot of talk about Congressman Garfield's coming visit to Riverton as well as about the capture of the Big Foot Gang. After an hour of visiting, the families started leaving by ones and twos. Finally, there were only a few left.

The summer school group of Angus McTavish, Betty Jones, Harry Acker, Wilma Sue Bevins, Audrey and Brad came down from the balcony.

"Wilma Sue, you know everything," said Audrey.

"I know, but I get so nervous when I take a test, I can't remember what I studied."

"You'll do better from now on," commented Brad. "If you do all, or most, of your studying the night before the test, you'll have trouble on the test. Study every night and talk about what you've studied. That will make it easier to remember."

"You can prepare for the test too," added Audrey. "Ask yourself questions about what you've studied and then answer the questions. That will also help make the test easier."

CHAPTER 9
CONGRESSMAN GARFIELD ARRIVES

It was Tuesday morning, a little before half past seven, when Harold Benton rode up to the sheriff's Office. He dismounted and wrapped the reins over the hitching rail.

"You're the second one to arrive," said Sheriff Tate as he welcomed Harold Benton into his office. "David Acker got here about ten minutes ago with a big container of hot coffee."

"Have a cup," said David as he handed a large cup to Harold.

"Thanks, David; it's still a bit chilly in the morning." Warming his hands with the cup, he looked at the sheriff and asked, "How many men do you have lined up to help this morning?"

"Let's see; I've got you, David, Bear, Jake, and Rob Wesley. That makes six of us. Six should be more than enough."

"David, this is really good coffee," said Harold.

"Thanks. It's a special hotel blend I get from New Orleans."

The door opened, and Jake Jackson entered exclaiming exuberantly, "It is a be-u-teee-ful day. It is a great day for our future president to come to Riverton."

"He's not the president yet," advised David Acker. "The election is still months away, and the Republican Convention doesn't begin until next week. His party hasn't even nominated a candidate."

"He would be an excellent candidate," acknowledged Sheriff Tate. "I was with him at Chickamauga in 1862 and later in 1863 in Chestertown, Maryland. He really knows how to handle people. In Chestertown, General Garfield was giving a speech in favor of abolition. Some rebel sympathizers started throwing eggs at him. He stopped his speech and announced, 'I have just come from fighting brave rebels at Chickamauga; I shall not flinch before cowardly rebels.'"

"Very prudent comment," said David. "He called the Confederate soldiers brave men. That way he didn't alienate those folks sympathetic with the South. But he really humiliated the egg throwers by calling them cowards. What happened to the egg throwers?"

"They left, and the General finished his speech."

"I see why you think he would be an excellent candidate," concluded Mr. Acker.

"He knows how to handle a mob too," added Harold. "I was with him on April 15, 1865, just after President Lincoln was assassinated. We were at the Exchange Building in New York City when word of Lincoln's assassination reached New York. A mob assembled outside crying 'Vengeance.' A number of men tried unsuccessfully to dissuade the mob from attacking the Democratic newspaper, the *New York World*. Congressman Garfield went to the balcony, raised his arm, and gave this brief speech to the mob."

Harold raised his right arm and in a booming voice said:

> *Fellow citizens! Clouds and darkness are round about Him! His pavilion is dark waters and thick clouds of the skies! Justice and judgment are the establishment of His throne! Mercy and truth shall go before His face! Fellow citizens! God reigns and the Government at Washington still lives!*

"How do you know the words?" asked the sheriff.

"I remembered most of the words because it was a terrifying situation. Thousands of men armed with sticks, screaming for vengeance. He turned a riotous mob into a prayer meeting."

"That would make most folks remember the speech," agreed Mr. Acker.

"A reporter copied the congressman's words," said Harold. "His speech was printed in the newspaper, and I bought a copy of it. I read the article many times. Garfield's little speech prevented a riot. He'll make a good president -— if he's nominated and elected."

Sheriff Tate held up his hand, and the men stopped talking. They looked at the horses stopping in front. Sheriff Tate looked out the window and announced, "Reverend Wesley and Bear are here; that's all my deputies."

Bear opened the door and entered the sheriff's office. As usual, his six-foot three-inch frame and two hundred-forty pounds seemed to fill the room and there was a momentary silence. The reverend entered after Bear, looked around the office and said, "Thank you for getting their attention, Bear. Now the service can begin."

"I see what you mean," said the sheriff with a wink to the reverend. "The room does quiet down when he enters."

Reverend Wesley had a Colt Peacemaker strapped on. The bottom of the holster was easily visible below his coat. The pistol looked out of place with his clerical collar and coat.

"I didn't know you carried a gun, Reverend," commented David Acker looking at the reverend's Peacemaker.

"I usually don't," he said pushing his unbuttoned coat back so that his pistol could be seen. "But I was a deputy before I went to seminary. I learned very quickly that when a person wears a badge, he'd better wear a gun. Folks generally do what you tell them when you're wearing both."

"I don't think we'll have any need for guns today," said Sheriff Tate. "But the reverend's right; when you wear a badge, you should wear a gun."

Jake Jackson finished his coffee and nodded in agreement, "That's right. Besides, if'n folks see the gun, you probably won't have to use it. That right, Sheriff?"

"Right, Jake."

"Any last minute word about Congressman Garfield?" asked Harold Benton.

"No new news," said the sheriff. "The train is still scheduled to arrive at nine o'clock. I want you men to work in pairs, stand at the edge of the crowd, and keep your eyes peeled. The Congressman has Pinkertons with him. I don't expect any trouble. Besides, just having some deputies at the station when Congressman Garfield gives his speech will probably be all the protection he needs."

"Sounds like a quiet morning," said David.

"That just what I want, a quiet morning," replied the sheriff.

"How are the varmints in your jail getting along?" asked Jake.

The sheriff smiled and said, "Curly and Clete were surprised to find Zeke, Clay, and Slade in jail. They thought Big Foot had eaten them. None of them want to go back to the Big Foot Mine. It seems they're afraid of Big Foot."

"That's good," said Jake Jackson. "If they cause problems, I'll help Hank Lacy take 'em back to the mine."

"Oh, they complained a little bit about the food Sunday evening. But that stopped when Marshal Cole stopped in with a prisoner Monday morning who had spent time in the State prison. I can't remember his name, but he told the men what to expect, including the food they'd receive. I haven't gotten a complaint since. Why, Zeke even asked to speak to the reverend last night."

"Slade summed it up very well," said Reverend Wesley. "He said the prisoner had spent five years at State. The prisoners usually get a bowl of mush and a cup of weak coffee for breakfast. The coffee is not like the Riverton Hotel coffee. Lunch is almost always soup, bread, and water. The evening meal is usually stew, and sometimes some fruit. Those that do what they're told and don't cause problems may get on a work detail. If they're on a work detail, they usually get a good lunch.

So, the smart prisoners don't cause problems and do what they're told so they can get on a work detail."

The sheriff looked at the wall clock and announced, "It's half past eight, time for us to get going. Jake, you go with David. Bear, work with the reverend. Harold, you're my partner. Let's go to the depot."

Sheriff Tate and his deputies arrived at the depot at a quarter to nine. The sheriff assigned the men the areas they were to watch as the citizens of Riverton began to arrive. When the special train chugged into Riverton, the engineer stopped the engine at the far end of the depot so that the last car was in the center of the crowd. Four Pinkertons exited from the first car and mixed with the crowd. A few minutes later Congressman Garfield stepped onto the rear platform of the last car and the crowd applauded.

"We've got trouble," said the sheriff. "Jimmy Ledbetter has just arrived, and he's drunker than a steer on loco weed. Let's take him off to jail so he can sleep it off. No need to let him cause a problem for Riverton."

Sheriff Tate and Harold walked up to Jimmy. Harold took Jimmy's left arm, and the sheriff took his right arm. "Let's go, Jimmy."

"Sheriff," he whined, "I ain't done nothin'; I just come to see what was happenin'. Please don't put me in jail."

"I'm taking you in for your own good, Jimmy. You haven't done anything wrong, and I don't want you to. I'll let you sleep in your favorite cell. I'll get you up for lunch; then you can go home. How does that sound?"

"Free lunch," slurred Jimmy, "just for sleeping in my favorite cell. Sure."

Sheriff Tate left Jimmy in Harold Benton's charge

and went back to the depot. Jimmy walked with Harold's help toward the jail.

"What's happenin' at the depot, Mr. Benton?"

"Congressman Garfield is giving a speech. He's on his way to the Republican Convention in Chicago. He'll tell folks that the Republicans will nominate a great man for Presidency of the United States. So he's coming to Riverton to tell the folks what a great president the Republican nominee will be."

Harold helped Jimmy step up to the boardwalk in front of the sheriff's office. Jimmy staggered as he entered the office, but Harold's firm support kept him from falling.

"We're here. I'll open the cell," said Harold.

As Jimmy entered the cell he asked, "Why can't I hear his speech?"

"Because you're drunk, Jimmy. When you're drunk you ask dumb questions and shout at folks."

"I only shout so they can hear me. If I don't shout, they don't answer," whined Jimmy.

"Well, if you were to shout during the Senator's speech, I'd have to arrest you for disturbing the peace. Do you want to pay a fine and spend a few days in jail?" asked Harold.

"No."

"That's why I'm letting you sleep off your drink, Jimmy. I don't want you to be arrested and have to pay a fine."

"Thanks, Mr. Benton." Jimmy flopped down on the bunk and quickly went to sleep.

The Big Foot Gang watched silently as Harold locked the cell door.

"You're a deputy?" asked Zeke.

"Only for today; Congressman Garfield is at the depot giving a campaign speech."

Harold left the sheriff's office and headed back to the depot. As he approached, he heard the train's whistle and the familiar chugs of an accelerating locomotive. The crowd was breaking up as the people went back to work or to their homes.

"Well, aren't you the lucky one," said Jake Jackson. "Congressman Garfield said we needed more folks like Brad, Audrey and Running Bear. Good folk risking their lives to capture the Big Foot Gang."

"He said that?" questioned Harold Benton.

"Sure did. But he also said he has been a great congressman and will be a great senator. That he'd support the Republican candidate for president. He got the folks all excited. If the Republicans make him their candidate, I expect he'll win the election."

"The election is months away. A lot can happen between now and then," predicted Mr. Acker.

Sheriff Tate and the rest of the deputies came to Harold and told him of Garfield's praise of Brad, Audrey, and Running Bear.

"Glad nothing happened," said the sheriff. "I don't count Jimmy being drunk as a big event. Have you talked to him about his drinking, Reverend?"

"I've tried, but he's not ready to quit. Maybe Zeke will succeed. Zeke has accepted the Lord. If Zeke talks to Jimmy about the Lord, he just might listen."

"Here's your badge, Sheriff," said Jake as he took off the badge and handed it to the sheriff.

"And mine, too," said David Acker as he looked at

some black clouds in the west. "It looks like we'll be getting some rain this afternoon."

Jake Jackson looked at the black clouds, and then back to Mr. Acker and said, "Looks like it'll be a real gully-washer too."

The rest of the deputies handed their badges over to the sheriff and left to go back to work.

"I'll see all of you at the trial," said David Acker as he started back to his hotel.

CHAPTER 10
CLETE COLLINS ESCAPES

It was late Wednesday afternoon, and Zeke sat on his bunk in the jail thinking about Jimmy Ledbetter. Clete Collins sat on his bunk on the other side of the cell.

Zeke thought to himself, *I hope I wasn't too hard on him. It's a shame the bottle has such a grip on him. He's a nice guy. My father wrecked his life drinking--froze to death in a snowstorm. He was so drunk; he couldn't open the door to get in the house.*

Zeke's thoughts were interrupted when Sheriff Tate announced, "Zeke, you have a visitor."

Zeke stood up and came to the bars of his cell door.

"Zeke, I came to thank you for talking to Jimmy Ledbetter," said Reverend Wesley.

"I don't understand, Reverend. Why should you thank me for talkin' to Jimmy?"

"As you know, Jimmy has a problem with liquor. When you told him how your father froze to death in a snowstorm, he finally accepted the fact that he had a problem. He came to me last night and asked for help. It seems that last winter, Jimmy himself nearly froze to death in a snowstorm. Fortunately, Sheriff Tate found him asleep in the alley and put him in jail for the night."

139

"Well, I did tell 'im about my Pa's drinking and freezing to death. Glad I could help, Reverend."

"I'd like to help you, Zeke. Are you a Christian?"

"I don't rightly know. I might be. My Ma read to me from the Bible when I was a kid. Even took me to church. When I was eight years old, the consumption got her, and she died. Pa said he didn't believe in that church stuff. I went alone once, but Pa found out and whupt me. Pa told me to never go again. He said I didn't need no churchin'."

"Your Pa didn't know it, but everyone needs some kind of churching. The Lord doesn't make people come to church, but he welcomes those that do come to hear his word. May I tell you about the Lord?"

"I'd like that, Reverend. My Ma said I should follow the Lord, but I never knew what she meant."

Reverend Wesley explained what Zeke's mother had meant about following the Lord.

"Ma always said I was to 'do unto others as I'd have them to do unto me.' What did she mean, Reverend?"

"Well, have you ever had anything taken from you?

Zeke thought a moment and then said, "When I was about ten years old I'd been fishin' and caught a nice string a' trout for dinner. Some big kids took my fish. I put up a fight, but I lost. There was two of 'em, and they really beat me up."

"How did you feel about that?"

"I was real angry and went to bed hungry. Those fish were goin' to be my dinner. I never saw those big kids again."

"Zeke, what your Ma meant was really quite simple. You didn't like those big kids taking your fish, so you

140

shouldn't take someone else's fish. That carries over to the rest of your life. You shouldn't take things that don't belong to you."

"You said the Lord forgives. Will he forgive me for stealin'?"

"He will forgive you if you ask him. You will still be punished, but he will forgive you."

"Here's your dinner," said the sheriff, setting a big pot of stew on the floor.

Clete suddenly saw a way to escape. Carefully he pulled a small knife from the inside of his boot and tucked it in his belt. Reverend Wesley had his hands on the bars as he talked to Zeke. Clete walked up behind Zeke as if he was going to say something to the reverend. With his right hand, he threw Zeke and into the wall and grabbed Reverend Wesley with his left hand. Pulling the reverend against the bars, he put the knife to the reverend's throat.

"Sheriff!" commanded Clete. "Open this door or the reverend gets to say hello to his Lord right now."

Sheriff Tate stared in astonishment at the knife on the reverend's throat. "Don't kill him. I'll open the door."

Sheriff Tate unlocked the door and stepped back. Clete smiled and gave another command, "Take off your gunbelt and drop it on the floor."

Sheriff Tate again did as Clete ordered.

"Clete, don't hurt the reverend," said Zeke. "He ain't done nothin'."

"He won't get hurt if the sheriff's smart. Sheriff, are you smart enough to get on that bunk with Zeke?"

Clete slowly opened the cell door. The sheriff carefully entered the cell and sat on the bunk with Zeke.

"Now, be real quiet, and the reverend won't get hurt," snarled Clete.

Clete threw Reverend Wesley into the jail wall next to Zeke, hurried out of the cell, turned, and slammed the cell door closed. Then he picked up the sheriff's gunbelt and keys. As he locked the door he said, "I'll leave your gun in the office with the keys. Count to 100 slowly before you think about calling for help. If you holler too soon, I may help you with some hot lead."

Clete put the sheriff's gunbelt and keys on the desk. He opened the desk drawers until he found his own gunbelt. As he strapped it on, he pulled his rifle from the rack and went to the side door of the sheriff's office. Clete slowly opened the door and quietly entered the deserted alley. Acting very confident, he straightened his hat and walked toward the livery.

"Evening, Ma'am," said Clete as he tipped his hat to an elderly woman.

Clete entered the livery and found his horse. *I'll take my own horse. I certainly don't want to be accused of being a horse thief.*

He saddled his horse, led it out of the livery, and headed south. *I've got a friend outside of Denver who'll put me up for a while,* he said to himself. *I'll go to his spread.*

"Richard," said Miss Jones, "are you here?"

"I'm in the jail, Stacey. Are the keys on my desk?"

"Yes."

"Please bring them to me."

Stacey picked up the keys and turned the corner to bring them to the sheriff.

"Richard," she exclaimed, "what are you doing in that cell?"

"Clete Collins held a knife to the reverend's throat. Said he'd kill him if I didn't let him out. Unlock the cell door so I can form a posse."

Stacey unlocked the cell door as the sheriff examined the unconscious reverend.

"The reverend's hurt," said Zeke. "He needs a doctor."

"That is a nasty gash on his head," observed the sheriff. "Can you carry him alone?"

"He ain't that heavy, and I owe 'im," declared Zeke. "I won't try to escape."

"Pick him up and let's go," ordered the sheriff.

"I'll run ahead and let Doc Adams know Reverend Wesley has been hurt and that you're bringing him up," said Miss Jones.

Zeke picked up Reverend Wesley, placed him over his right shoulder, and carried him out of the cell. Sheriff Tate, his hand on his pistol, opened the office door and followed Zeke out the door. The reverend groaned as Zeke climbed the stairs to Doc Adam's office. Miss Jones had the door open, and the doctor was at the examining table.

Doc Adams looked at the reverend on Zeke's shoulder. "Place him on the table. What happened to him?"

"Clete threw him against the jail wall," replied Zeke.

Doc Adams carefully cleaned the wound on the reverend's forehead. "He'll have a knot on his head for awhile, but he'll probably be okay."

Reverend Wesley's eyes slowly opened. "Did Clete escape?" he asked.

"Not for long," said the sheriff. "I'll get a few men and get on his trail right away."

"I'll take care of the reverend. You get your men together and find Clete," said Miss Jones. "We can have dinner together tomorrow night."

"What in tarnation's goin' on?" asked Jake Jackson as he entered the doctor's office.

"Clete Collins escaped from jail," said Miss Jones.

"Jake, can you find a couple of good men to help me track him? We need to leave right away," said the sheriff.

"I can git ya' two good men and a good girl; Brad and Audrey Benton just rode in. They're at the stage office with their father."

"Zeke," asked the sheriff, "did Clete say anything that might help us?"

"No, sir, he just sat on his bunk and stared. He wouldn't talk to us."

"Zeke!" exclaimed Jake. "He's one of the polecats what robbed the stage. He's supposed to be in jail!"

"He was until the reverend got hurt. Are ready to go back, Zeke?"

"Reckon so, Sheriff; pleased to have met you, Miss Jones."

Sheriff Tate took Zeke back to the jail while Jake went to the stage office to get the Bentons.

"Mr. Benton, Audrey, Brad," said Jake, "the sheriff needs you right away. Clete Collins just escaped."

"Pa, I'll take you to the livery for your horse," offered Audrey.

"Brad, will ya' take me to my place so I can git my horse?" asked Jake.

"Sure."

"We'll meet at the sheriff's office," said their father.

Harold Benton dismounted and entered the livery with his daughter. "Need a good horse right away, Alex. Clete Collins just escaped."

"That explains why his horse and saddle are missing," responded Alex. "I'll give you the big black. He hasn't been ridden for a few days. He's got lots of stamina."

"I'll get the saddle," said Harold Benton.

While they saddled the black, Alex recounted, "I rented out Clete's horse this morning. Len Reno's horse was lame, so he rented Clete's horse for the day. Said he rode her hard all day long. Just as he was coming into Riverton, she started favoring her right front hoof. He checked it and took out a rock. She favored that hoof even after he took out the rock, so Clete's horse is tired and lame. But he probably won't find that out for a bit."

"That's good to know. Thanks, Alex," said Harold.

Audrey and her father left the livery and headed back to the sheriff's office. Sheriff Tate, Jake Jackson and Brad were mounted and ready to go.

"Brad believes Clete will probably head back to the Denver area," said the sheriff. "Since the jail's on the south side of town, he probably headed south. He's too smart to ride down Main Street after escaping from jail. Once out of town, he'll feel safe. Then he'll circle around the town and head north to Denver."

"He took his horse and saddle from the livery," added Harold. "It looks like Brad's theory might be correct.

What Clete doesn't know is that his horse is tired and probably lame. Alex rented his horse to Len Reno this morning, and she got a rock in her right front hoof. She favored that hoof even after he took out the rock."

Sheriff Tate pondered for a moment and then predicted, "Once out of Riverton, he'll probably take the valley road west, and then cut north. If he does that, he'll have to go through Mustang Gap."

"Sheriff, how about you and Jake follow him south," suggested Harold Benton. "I'll take Audrey and Brad and set up an ambush at Mustang Gap. Jim Bates is getting his horse and should be here shortly. If we're right, Clete will ride right into our hands. We'll see you at Mustang Gap."

"Mustang Gap is just ahead," said Audrey. "Now we have to think of a good way to capture Clete."

"He's a crafty criminal, and he's armed," said her father. "We don't want him to have a chance to use his guns."

"We have to let him come to us," stated Brad. "We want to make him enter our trap."

"Let's do the same thing to him that he did to my stage," said Jim Bates. "The rain Tuesday caused flash flooding that uprooted some small trees and bushes. We can tie a rope around them and pull them onto the trail by that boulder. He'll probably ride between those two giant boulders to get back to the trail."

"And that's where we'll get him, just like a steer in a chute," declared Brad.

"Steer in a chute?" questioned Audrey.

"Remember the roundup at the Bar-X last year? The men herded the cattle into that small box canyon. The draw got so narrow that only one steer could go through it at a time. Hank had them rope and brand the cattle one at a time. That made the roundup real easy."

"And we'll be able to hog-tie Clete just like a steer in that box canyon's draw," agreed Audrey.

"Sounds simple," replied her father. "I hope it works."

"Mr. Bates, I'll help you bring those uprooted bushes," said Brad. "I'll tie a rope to them and let Ebony drag them to the trail."

"I'll get up in those rocks and find the best position to cover him with my rifle," said Harold Benton. "We may not have much time."

Brad and Jim Bates pulled several uprooted bushes onto the trail. Then they added a few large rocks.

"The trail looks like a flash flood blocked it," said Brad. "But he could always decide to ride through it rather than between those two giant boulders."

"Not if there's a rattlesnake there," said Audrey.

"Most of the rattlesnakes I've met haven't been too cooperative. How do we get one to come and curl up in the bushes?" asked Jim Bates.

"Easy," said Audrey. "I have one in my saddlebag."

"It's the baby rattle for Mrs. Simpson's new baby!" exclaimed Brad.

"I don't want you in those bushes," warned Jim. "He might decide to shoot at the rattler thinking he can scare it away."

"We'll tie it to one of the bushes," explained Audrey. "I'll tie a rawhide thong to the bush. Then I can stand behind that big tree and pull the thong. He won't be able to see me. If he decides to shoot, he'll shoot at the bush, not the big tree I'll be hiding behind."

"Let's hook up that baby rattle and see if it works," said Jim.

In a few minutes, the baby rattle was tied to the bush, and two rawhide thongs were tied to the branch with the rattle.

"When you pull them back and forth rapidly, it sounds just like a rattler," confirmed Brad.

"I've got my rope across the chute at neck level," said Jim. "It's getting dark, and it'll be hard to see. We should be able to knock him to the ground before he knows what happened."

"A rider's coming," warned Harold Benton. "He's about a mile away. Brad, take the horses and tether them in that stand of trees."

"Everyone in their places," ordered Jim. "Don't make a sound. We don't want any shooting if we can avoid it."

Clete Collins let out a spate of oaths about his lame horse. *Just my rotten luck, my horse is lame. Good thing I covered my trail by riding for miles through rocks and up that little creek. No one could follow me, except maybe an Apache scout. One thing's for sure, those Riverton bumpkins will be totally lost. It'll take them weeks to figure out where I'm going.*

Clete approached Mustang Gap and noticed the bushes in the trail. *There must have been a flash flood that washed those bushes into the trail. I'll just have to go ride through them.*

As Clete approached the bushes, Audrey started pulling the rawhide thongs to the baby rattle.

"What in blazes?" stammered Clete. "It must be a

rattler. I'm not going to tangle with a rattler. I'll loop up between those boulders and catch the trail on the other side."

Clete reined his horse to the right and entered the chute between the two giant boulders. "Agggh!" was all Clete could utter as the rope hit his neck. He was leaning way back in the saddle and pulling back on the reins when Brad hit the rump of his horse with a small rock. The horse spooked and bolted down the trail. Clete slammed onto the ground. The fall knocked the wind out of him. It took him half a minute to regain it. He started to stand up when he felt something poke him in the back.

"Don't move," warned Jim. "You're also covered by my partner with a rifle. He's in the rocks to your right."

"That's right," confirmed Harold Benton. "I've got you covered, too."

"Now I want you to stick your hands out, real slow like, and count to 100 as my assistant ties your hands."

Brad pulled his hat down on his face and carefully approached Clete with some rawhide. He quickly tied Clete's hands and then stepped back.

"Now, put your hands up as high as you can and face that boulder," commanded Jim Bates.

Clete did as ordered. He still didn't realize who had captured him. "I don't have any money, and my horse is lame. You'll do better robbing someone else."

"Don't talk, just do as I say. Now, I want you to keep your hands on the boulder and move your feet back from the boulder. Now!" ordered Jim.

Clete did as ordered. "I can't move my feet back any more without falling," complained Clete.

"Good," said Jim. "Now my partner will search you."

Brad unbuckled Clete's gunbelt and put it on a boulder about ten feet behind Jim. Then he checked Clete's boots and removed a knife. While Brad was searching Clete, Harold had come down to join his children and Jim Bates.

"Is that the knife you held to the reverend's throat?" asked Harold Benton.

Clete was shocked when he realized who his captors were. "How did you know I was coming this way?" barked Clete.

"That's easy," answered Brad. "Most criminals make mistakes. That's why they get caught. Ask Sheriff Tate if you wish; he's just arrived."

"I see you caught our robber again," said the sheriff, reining his horse to a halt.

"It's the jail agin' fer you, you polecat," declared Jake. "And the reverend better be okay, or I'll skin ya' alive."

"I'll get his horse. Did you get the rattler?" asked Brad.

"Yes, it's right here," replied his sister.

"That's just a baby rattle," exclaimed Clete.

"True, but it sounded enough like a real rattler to get you to come through this chute," giggled Audrey.

"Let's get out of here before dark," cautioned the sheriff. "I don't want to stay here any longer than necessary. Big Foot might still be in the area."

"Here's his horse," said Brad. "I'll tie his hands to the saddle horn."

Harold Benton kept Clete covered as Jim Bates helped Brad tie Clete's hands to the saddle horn.

"Sorry your horse is lame, but we'll take it easy on the way back," said the sheriff. "If we're lucky, Big Foot will be at his cave and won't bother us. Let's mount up and head back to Riverton."

Audrey put the baby rattle back in her saddlebag. Then they mounted their horses.

"Brad, Audrey, you take the lead," said the sheriff. "You two have the best eyes, then your father and Clete. Jake and I'll take the rear."

A full moon and a clear sky made the ride back to Riverton rather easy. The occasional hoot of an owl broke the night air, as did the distant howling of some wolves. Brad and Audrey talked with Jake about Big Foot, which caused Clete to look anxiously around for signs of the 400-pound furry critter.

It was just after dark when the small posse arrived at the jail. "If'n that furry critter had come after us, I'da cut ya' off that horse," said Jake. "Better he eats you than one of us."

"Untie his hands from the saddle," said the sheriff.

Brad freed Clete from the saddle horn and Jim Bates prodded him up the steps to the jail.

"That was a quick trip, Richard," observed Miss Jones. "I imagine you've worked up quite an appetite. If you'd like, we can still have dinner at the hotel."

"I'm starved," remarked the sheriff. "But first, I have to put this critter back in his cell."

Clete went through the front door of the sheriff's office and back to the cells. Sheriff Tate opened the cell door.

"This is your cell, Clete. I'll bring you something to eat tomorrow morning." The sheriff paused at length and continued, "That will be after I visit the reverend. You weren't here for tonight's dinner."

Jake shut the cell door, and Clete put his hands through the bars. Sheriff Tate untied the rawhide strips and Clete went to his bunk, sat down, and rubbed his wrists.

"You didn't need to hurt the reverend," challenged Zeke. "He didn't hurt you."

"If'n ya' do that again, I'll hog-tie ya' in Big Foot's cave," declared Jake.

"Feed him to Big Foot," agreed Clay. "It'd serve him right for hurtin' the reverend."

"Yeah, he could've let us out too," added Slade. "Feed him to Big Foot."

Sheriff Tate and Jake went to the front of the office. They could hear Clete's partners giving him a rough time.

"We took the horses to the livery for you, Sheriff," said Brad.

"Have a nice dinner with Miss Jones," said Audrey.

"You two Pinkertons helped me again," said the sheriff. "Thank you."

"Victoria has dinner waiting for us," said their father. "Let's mount up and get home. See you tomorrow, Richard."

Abby Benton and Victoria heard the horses and rushed to the front door. Abby held the lantern as they stood on the front porch.

"Abby, Victoria, sorry we're late," announced Harold Benton.

"I'll hold the lantern while you take care of the horses," said Abby. "What happened?"

Brad and his father removed the saddles while Audrey brought some horse towels.

"Clete Collins escaped this evening," explained her husband. "We helped Sheriff Tate capture him. Clete is once again sitting in the Riverton jail. And," he continued, "Miss Jones and the sheriff are having dinner at the Riverton Hotel."

Audrey wiped down Blaze as Brad and her father put the saddles in the tack room.

"I got the rattle for Mrs. Simpson's new baby," said Audrey. "It's a good one. It even made Clete believe that it was a rattlesnake."

"Clete thought it was a rattlesnake?" questioned her mother. "Couldn't he see you shaking it?"

"I hid the rattle in the bushes," giggled Audrey. He couldn't see it."

"I don't know about you two," said Abby Benton. "First, you make the robbers believe in Big Foot. And now, you make one of them think a baby rattle is a rattlesnake."

"Well, we've got the horses taken care of. Let's have dinner," said Harold Benton.

Abby held the lantern high as the four of them walked up to the house. Victoria had set the table and was bringing in the food as they entered the front door.

"Wash up and come eat. Dinner's not hot, but it's still warm," announced Victoria.

The three Bentons washed their face and hands at the kitchen pump and then sat down at the dining room table. Harold Benton said grace and started serving the plates.

"Enough of this silence, Harold P. Tell me what

happened. And this time, don't tell me it was Big Foot," chided Victoria.

"It wasn't Big Foot, it was Brad."

"I did what Running Bear said to do," Brad responded. "I put myself in Clete's shoes and asked myself what he'd do. Clete probably has friends in the Denver area, so I figured that he'd go north."

"But he'd also want to get out of town as fast as possible," added Audrey. "Since the livery and the jail are on the south side of Riverton, he'd go south. Once out of town he'd head north through the rocky flats to Denver."

Victoria pondered what Brad and Audrey had said for a moment. Cocking her head and closing her left eye, she asked, "And just how did you track him through the rocks so fast?"

"We didn't," replied Harold Benton. "We guessed he'd probably go west, and then north."

"That meant he'd go through Mustang Gap," confirmed Audrey. "We went north and set up an ambush for him at Mustang Gap. He walked right into it."

"Actually, he rode into it," explained Brad. "We put a rope across the trail, and I hit his horse's rump with a rock when he hit the rope."

"He was flat on the ground," chuckled their father. "Never knew what hit him. Jim Bates was prodding him with a rifle before he could stand up. Jim had him hold his hands out and count to 100, very slowly. While he was counting, Brad tied his hands. I believe you call that poetic justice."

"The poor man, he didn't have a chance against you," said Abby. "I'm glad no one was hurt."

"Is the trial still set for Friday?" asked Victoria.

"No reason to change the date," replied Harold. "All the robbers are still in jail."

"It's late, and you've got to get to work tomorrow," said Abby. "Everyone do their chores and then to bed."

Brad and Audrey started the dishes as their mother and grandmother cleared the table. Harold Benton filled the woodbox and the lanterns.

"I'm tired," whispered Audrey to her brother. "But I still want to go to the creek for a swim tomorrow."

"In the afternoon," replied Brad. "I'll be sleeping in tomorrow morning."

"You mean you won't be up at the crack of dawn to see your horse," said Nana.

"Ebony needs to sleep too," said Brad. "No horses tomorrow, just swimming."

CHAPTER 11
THE TRIAL

The trial of the Big Foot Gang began Friday morning at the Riverton Hotel. Judge Callahan convened court and listened to the charges against the members of the gang. Zeke, Slade, Clay, and Curly pled guilty to the charges and asked for leniency. They also admitted to making a Big Foot costume so they could blame future robberies on Big Foot.

Sheriff Tate testified that the four men had been polite and cooperative while awaiting trial. Running Bear testified that he had offered to assist Sheriff Tate in taking the men to the Big Foot Mine to search for additional evidence. However, the four men did not want burden Sheriff Tate, and agreed to plead guilty.

"Slade Finnegan, Clay Overman, and Curly Pflug," said Judge Callahan, "by your own admission, you are guilty of robbing the Overland stage. I hereby sentence each of you to one year in the state prison. If you had not pled guilty and been so cooperative with Sheriff Tate, your sentence would have been more severe."

Slade, Clay, and Curly sighed with relief. They had expected a longer sentence.

"Zeke Bushman," said Judge Callahan, "by your own admission, you are guilty of robbing the Overland stage. However, you helped Sheriff Tate by carrying the reverend to Doc Adams office. I hereby sentence you to six months in the state prison. If you had not helped Sheriff Tate after Clete Collin's escape, your sentence would have been more severe."

"Clete Collins, the court finds you guilty of planning and committing the robbery, threatening an officer of the law and violently assaulting Reverend Wesley. I hereby sentence you to five years in the state prison. Sheriff Tate, take charge of the prisoners. Court dismissed."

Judge Callahan banged his gavel and the people who had watched the trial immediately began talking to each other. Sheriff Tate and his deputies, Jake Jackson and Hank Lacy, started to escort the prisoners back to the jail. As the prisoners neared the door, Zeke stopped in front of Reverend Wesley.

"Reverend," said Zeke, "Thanks for talking to me about the Lord. When I get out of prison, may I come see you?"

"Of course; I'll even help you find a job."

Hank Lacy looked at the reverend and said, "Reverend, if you vouch for Zeke, I'll give him a job when he gets out of prison. I can always use a good hand, especially when the reverend recommends him."

"Mr. Lacy," said Zeke, "I'd really appreciate that. I'll write the reverend and let him know when I'm getting out."

"Zeke, thanks again for talking to Jimmy Ledbetter," said Reverend Wesley.

"Zeke, if you keep doing good things while you're in prison, I'll talk to the governor about letting you out early," said Harold Benton.

Zeke looked at Hank, Harold, and the reverend and said excitedly, "I'll do that. It made me feel good to help Jimmy Ledbetter. Maybe I can help some folks in prison like I helped Jimmy. I'll get a Bible and read it every day."

"If you're going to do that, I'll send you a Bible," said a man behind Reverend Wesley.

Hank and Harold turned around with the reverend to see who had offered the Bible.

"My name's George Scott and this is Henry Morris," he said nodding to the man beside him. "We're from the Overland Stage Company. I know the warden at the state prison. I'll send him a Bible and ask him to give it to you."

Sheriff Tate and Hank escorted the prisoners out of the hotel lobby. Brad and Audrey were at the hotel desk talking with Miss Jones and Running Bear.

George Scott continued, "We're looking for Brad and Audrey Benton, and Running Bear. I believe Brad and Audrey are related to you. We're here to present the reward to them and to Running Bear."

Harold Benton beamed with pride as he escorted Mr. Scott and Mr. Morris over to his children and Running Bear.

"This is Running Bear, and these are my children, Brad and Audrey."

George Scott smiled and said, "On behalf of Overland Stage Company, I wish to thank the three of you for helping capture the Big Foot Gang. I have a draft which I can present to the Bank of Riverton for two thousand dollars."

"The bank is right around the corner, Mr. Scott. We

can go right now," said Harold Benton motioning them to the front door.

As they were walking to the bank, George Scott asked, "Mr. Benton, did your children really help capture the Big Foot Gang?"

"They did, with the help of Running Bear. They tracked the gang to the old Big Foot Mine, and Audrey rode into Riverton for the sheriff. Running Bear let himself be captured by one of the robbers so Brad could stay free. After Bear was captured, Brad snuck into the mine and knocked out the robber that was guarding Bear. Then Brad and Bear captured two more of the robbers before the sheriff and his posse arrived at the mine. Later, Audrey and Running Bear disarmed Clete Collins who had tied up Sheriff Tate, Brad, and me."

"I understand you also recaptured Clete Collins after he escaped," said Mr. Morris.

"That's right," said Brad. "It was easy. We just did what Running Bear taught us to do."

"And what was that?" asked Mr. Scott.

"I put myself in Clete's shoes and asked myself what he would do," said Brad. "Even though he went south when he left town, I figured that he'd go north to Denver later."

"You learned well," said Running Bear.

"I'm very proud of what my children and Bear accomplished," said Harold Benton.

"You certainly should be," said George Scott as they entered the bank. "Let's see the bank president, and I'll present the reward. Of course, you'll have to certify that the reward was paid. Your children and Running

Bear will have to sign that they received the money. And, uh, it's okay if Running Bear makes an X."

"That won't be necessary," laughed Harold. "Running Bear is a graduate of the Riverton Bible College. After he graduated, he taught English at the college for a few years. Now he's the teacher at the Indian school, ten miles northwest of Riverton."

Mr. Scott's face briefly flushed with embarrassment for presuming that Bear was illiterate. Turning to Bear he said, "Running Bear, please accept my apologies for implying that you could not read or write English. I was trying to prevent an embarrassing situation for you, but instead managed to embarrass myself."

Running Bear smiled and said, "I appreciate your concern. An apology is not necessary." Then a smile covered his face and as he continued. "Or should I say, me no mean cause problem by write name. Me heap big sorry."

Mr. Scott and the Bentons laughed at Bear's imitation of an Indian with little knowledge of the English language. The bank's president, David Goldman, saw the group with the Bentons and strode across the lobby to them.

"Mr. Benton, may I help you?"

"Yes, you may. These gentlemen are from the Overland Stage Company. This is George Scott, and this is Henry Morris. They have a bank draft to cash. It's the reward for capturing the Big Foot Gang."

"This will take a few minutes," said Mr. Goldman looking at the draft. "Come into my office while I take this to our head cashier."

The group was ushered into Mr. Goldman's office. A few minutes later, he joined them.

"Audrey, Brad, Bear," said Mr. Goldman, "I can give you cash if you wish, but it would be safer if you deposited the money in the bank until you need it. What do you want to do?"

Bear spoke first. "I'd like fifty dollars now for the school-fixing barbecue on Saturday. I'll deposit the remaining nine hundred fifty dollars in the bank. I'll use it for books and school supplies later this year."

"We'd like to deposit our thousand dollars in the bank too," said Audrey. "We need more time to decide how to wisely use the money."

Mr. Goldman smiled and said, "This reward money can be a real blessing for you, if you do use it wisely."

After the accounts were opened, deposits completed, and papers signed, the group left the bank. Running Bear thanked Mr. Scott and Mr. Morris for the reward, as did Brad and Audrey.

"I must go now," said Running Bear. "I have some supplies to get at the general store."

"And we must catch the noon stage back to Denver," said George Scott. "But before we leave, I want to let you know about a meeting in Denver this fall. We'll be bringing several station managers, like you, to Denver to discuss security. Overland is concerned about stagecoach robberies. There have been very few robberies in your area, and we want to keep it that way. We'll let you know as soon as the date is set. The meeting will probably be in October. Please plan on attending."

"I'll plan on coming. Just let me know the date,"

said Harold. "The stage is due in a few minutes, so we'd better get you to the stage office. Don't want to delay the departure."

The group arrived at the stage office just as the stage pulled up.

"Have a good trip," called Audrey as George Scott and Henry Morris climbed aboard the stage.

"And thanks again for the reward," yelled Brad as the stage departed.

"We've got to go home and do our chores, Pa," said Audrey as she and Brad mounted their horses.

"I'll see you tonight," he said as his two children urged their horses into a slow trot.

Early the next morning, Hank Lacy personally dug the pit and laid the fire to barbecue the steer. Running Bear and Lone Eagle prepared the steer for the barbecue while the men from the Bar-X repaired the school. After the repairs were completed, they had a lot of lumber and nails left over, so they built a small addition to the school. The Indian women filled a table with baked potatoes, carrots from the Benton's root cellar, fresh bread, and five of Victoria's apple-blackberry pies. David Acker donated some of the Riverton Hotel's special coffee, and Abby Benton made five gallons of lemonade.

Running Bear looked at Hank Lacy and the Bentons and said, "The school-fixing barbecue was a real success. Thank you."

"The pleasure is all ours, Bear," remarked Hank. "We thank you for helping stop the cattle rustling."

"Brad, Audrey," said their father. "Your mother and I are leaving now in the buggy. We'll see you at home."

Running Bear walked Brad and Audrey to their horses. "Thank you for helping my school. You are good Pinkertons and good trackers." Turning to Brad, he continued, "Thank you for rescuing me at the mine. I will not forget that you risked your life for me."

"I had to, Bear," said Brad, his voice choked and quavering. He continued, "You risked your life for me. I had to at least try to save you."

Audrey mounted Blaze and looked at her brother and said, "Nana is saving an apple-blackberry pie for us, Brad. I'll race you the last mile for the biggest piece."

"It's a deal Miss Pinkerton," said Brad as he mounted Ebony. "I'll race you the last country mile."

ADDENDUM ABOUT SASQUATCH

Sasquatch is the Anglicized (English) spelling of a Salish Indian word that loosely translates as "the wild man from the woods." The Salish is a native tribe in Canada. The common American term for Sasquatch has become Big Foot because of its best known characteristic, that being big feet.

Very few scientists, if any, acknowledge the existence of a Big Foot type of creature. Many scientists believe that reports of Big Foot are hoaxes or that people really saw something else, such as a bear. The fact that there have been many Big Foot hoaxes casts doubt on any reported sightings of a Big Foot that may be real.

Note that early reports of the Australian duck-billed platypus were rejected by scientists as hoaxes until the first duck-billed platypus was captured and examined by scientists. The legends of Big Foot will continue to be considered myths and reported sightings to be hoaxes until scientists find evidence to confirm they exist. This skepticism must be maintained, for it is a necessary foundation of science.

Legends about Big Foot, as well as reports from people who say they saw Big Foot, are consistent in many respects. Big Foot always walks upright and never walks on all fours like a bear. It has broad shoulders, a short neck, long arms, reddish-brown or black hair, big human-like feet, and a face like an ape. Big Foot's hands are human-like with fingers, not claws. It is reported to be six to eight feet tall and weigh three hundred to nine hundred pounds. The legends and sightings of Big Foot also report that it has a strong, almost intolerable odor.

Counterparts for the North American Big Foot include the Yeti in the Himalayan Mountains of Asia, the Almas in Russia's Siberia, and Ye Ren in China.

Over 2,500 people in the United States and Canada claim to have seen Big Foot. One of the most verifiable and convincing sightings was in 1967 by two men looking for evidence of Big Foot. Roger Patterson and Robert Gimlin filmed their sighting of Big Foot with a 16 mm movie camera. They filmed it for about a minute before they ran out of film. Some experts examined the film and concluded it was legitimate; other experts called the film a fraud.

In 1957 an elderly Canadian told about being captured by a family of Big Foot when he was in his twenties. The man related that he was held for six days, after which he managed to escape.

In 1941 some Russian Soldiers reported capturing a Big Foot, believing it might be a spy for Germany. Since Russia was fighting for survival from Hitler's invasion, no study of the creature was possible, and it was released.

In the 1840s, Reverend Elkanah Walker had a mission 265 miles northwest of Spokane, Washington.

Native tribes told him about a race of giants that lived in the mountains of perpetual snow.

In 1864, Alexander Anderson, a fur trader, was going through Fraser River canyon in Canada. He reported that he was attacked by several Big Foot creatures that tossed large rocks down upon him.

In 1868, the Boise, Idaho *Statesman* reported that a man claimed to have shot a Big Foot. Just before "Big Foot" died, he said that he was a human whose real name was "Nampuh." The city of Boise is relatively close to the city of Nampa, Idaho.

Legends of the Chippewa Indians of the Great Lakes area tell about a race of giant-sized cannibals that had a monstrous craving for human flesh. These cannibals were very strong and produced a very loud and piercing whistle.

An Ojibway Indian legend tells about a Big Foot that they call Windigo. The Windigo is not a cannibal, but is depicted as an ogre. The legend of the Windigo is used to scare naughty children into behaving.

ADDENDUM ABOUT THE NATIONAL HYMN
"GOD OF OUR FATHERS"

Daniel Roberts wrote the text of the hymn, "God of Our Fathers," for the 1876 centennial Fourth of July celebration in Brandon, Vermont. The first performance of the hymn was at his church, St. Thomas' Episcopal Church, in Brandon on that memorable date. The words were sung to the music of the "Russian Hymn," which is also the Russian National Anthem. Subsequently, probably in the late 1880s, Roberts sent the text to the Episcopal Church's Commission that was revising the Church's hymnal. The commission accepted his text for the 1892 edition of *The Hymnal Revised and Enlarged* of the Protestant Episcopal Church.

In 1892, Roberts' text was selected for the ceremony marking the centennial of the adoption of the United States Constitution. For that special occasion, George Warren, organist and choirmaster at New York City's St. Thomas Church, was commissioned by the Episcopal Church to compose the music that we know today as "God of Our Fathers." His arrangement introduced the hymn with a fanfare for three trumpets.

The early publications of "God of Our Fathers"

varied in several respects. The hymn as we know it was first published without trumpet fanfare under the title "America" in *The Hymnal Revised and Enlarged*, by Arthur Messiter, New York, 1892.

Two years later, in 1894, the hymn was published under the title "National Hymn" in *The Hymnal Revised and Enlarged* and again in 1897 under the name "Columbia" in James H. Darlington's *The Hymnal of the Church.*

A change to a hymn is not a phenomenon restricted to different publishers. In *The Hymnal of the Protestant Episcopal Church, 1940*, "God of Our Fathers" is number 143, and the original trumpet fanfare has been deleted. However, in the next edition of *The Hymnal of the Protestant Episcopal Church, 1982*, the hymn is number 718 and the original trumpet fanfare has been restored.

People are attracted to some hymns, without regard to their denominational heritage. "God of Our Fathers" is such a hymn. Originally Episcopalian, it has since been accepted by other churches and is included in their hymnals. It is truly a national hymn, but it is also a hymn of freedom that transcends religious and political boundaries throughout the world.

ADDENDUM ABOUT JAMES GARFIELD

James Garfield, the 20th president of the United States, was born in Orange Township, Ohio in 1831. His father, a canal worker and farmer, died when he was two years old. As was common in that era, his widowed mother continued working the farm with the help of her four children. James attended elementary school winters and worked the farm summers with his mother and brothers. As a teenager, he took a job driving the horse teams pulling canal boats on the Ohio and Erie Canals.

James Garfield entered Geauga Seminary in 1849 and became an ordained minister. Two years later, he entered what is now known as Hiram College, where he studied for three years. He then taught elementary school and held some other jobs. In 1854 he entered Williams College as a junior and graduated two years later.

He was elected to the Ohio State Senate in 1859. With the outbreak of the Civil War, he was commissioned as a Lieutenant Colonel in the Ohio Volunteer Infantry. On January 10, 1862, commanding a brigade as a colonel, he won a minor victory at Middle Creek, Kentucky and was promoted to brigadier general the next day.

In the summer of 1862, he was nominated as the Republican candidate for the U. S. House of Representatives. During that summer's campaign, he pledged to return to the battlefield after the election. After the election, he was appointed chief of staff of General William Rosecrans' Army of the Cumberland. General Rosecrans' Army drove the Confederates from Tennessee, but they failed to drive them from Georgia. The Union lost the battle of Chickamauga, Georgia, discrediting General Rosecrans. However, General Garfield's leadership in the battle was recognized, and he was promoted to the rank of major general.

Late in 1863, he resigned from the Army and took his seat in the U. S. House of Representatives, which he occupied until March 4, 1881.

On 15 April 1865, Congressman James Garfield was at Wall Street's Exchange Building in New York City when news of Lincoln's assassination reached the city. He calmed a mob crying "Vengeance" for the assassination of Abraham Lincoln. Garfield was a magnificent orator. He raised his arm and addressed the mob with these words:

> *Fellow citizens! Clouds and darkness are round about Him! His pavilion is dark waters and thick clouds of the skies! Justice and judgment are the establishment of His throne! Mercy and truth shall go before His face! Fellow citizens! God reigns and the Government at Washington still lives!*

The deeply moved mob dispersed. Congressman Garfield had prevented a riot.

In January, 1880, the Ohio State Legislature elected him to serve in the United States Senate beginning March 4, 1881. In 1880, the state legislatures elected their U. S. Senators; the public did not elect them.

At the 1880 Republican convention, he was nominated as the party's candidate for president on the 36th ballot. Garfield was elected President of the United States on November 2, 1880. Six days later, on November 8th, he resigned from the House of Representatives effective March 4, 1881, and surrendered his seat in the Senate effective March 4, 1881. Thus, on the date of his inauguration, March 4, 1881, James Garfield held three federal positions at the same time -- Congressman, Senator, and President. He is also the only U. S. President who was an ordained minister.

On July 2, 1881, after only four months in office, he was shot twice in the back by a disgruntled office seeker at the Baltimore & Potomac Railroad Station in Washington D.C. President Garfield's death after the shooting was needless. Unsanitary medical instruments and continual probing to find the bullets weakened him, eventually causing his death. Alexander Graham Bell, the inventor of the telephone, was asked to help find the bullet. Bell used his latest invention, an electrical listening device, to find the bullets, but was not successful. Garfield tenaciously clung to life until September 19, 1881 when he died at a seaside retreat in Elberon, New Jersey. He is buried at Lake View Cemetery, Cleveland, Ohio.

While President, Garfield openly investigated

corruption and mail contract fraud in the Post Office Department. The Post Office had huge debts, and for years it had asked Congress to appropriate additional funds. The Congress had done so, believing that it cost a lot of money to deliver mail in the rural United States. The *New York Times* newspaper investigated and discovered that thousands of dollars were being spent delivering mail to some places a few times each year. The *New York Times* called this the "Star Route Frauds."

President Garfield began a powerful reform movement that eventually changed the process of awarding government contracts and giving government positions as rewards for supporting a particular candidate.

BRAD AND AUDREY GO IN SEARCH OF THEIR FATHER WHO WAS TAKEN CAPTIVE.

FOR AN EXCERPT, TURN THE PAGE.

CHAPTER 2
BRAD DRIVES THE STAGECOACH

When the rumble of the horses' hooves had faded, Brad said, "They've shot Mr. Bates. We'd better check on him."

"Pa did everything they asked," cried his sister. "Why did they take him?"

"Because Duke Badger is an evil man," replied Brad. "I read about him and his gang in the *Denver Post* that Pa had in his office."

Brad and Audrey jumped out of the stage, rushed to the front, and looked up at Jim, who was pale with shock. "How badly are you hurt?" Brad asked as he climbed into the driver's seat.

"I'm bleeding pretty bad." Jim grimaced while he held his shoulder.

"Audrey, check those trees for some moss," said Brad. "We've got to stop the bleeding."

Brad pulled his kerchief out and pressed it against the bleeding wound. Audrey gathered some moss from a nearby tree and ran back to the stage.

"Here's the moss, Brad," she said fighting back her tears as she climbed up to them.

Brad had already removed the driver's shirt. He

pressed the moss against the wound and covered it with his kerchief.

"Audrey, I need some strips of cloth. Open Pa's bag and tear up one of his shirts. We'll wrap it around Mr. Bates' chest to keep the moss and kerchief pressed against the bullet hole."

Audrey grabbed her father's bag from the top of the stage, opened it, and removed a shirt. "Brad, I need your knife."

"Here," he said, handing her his pocketknife.

Audrey cut the edge of the shirt and began tearing it into strips. Then she tied the strips together to make them long enough to go around him. While pressing the moss and kerchief against the bleeding wound, Brad and Audrey wrapped the strips of cloth around the driver to hold the bandage tight. In a few minutes, the bandaging was complete.

"Mr. Bates, tell me how to turn the stage around so we can go back to Riverton," said Brad.

"Keep going up the hill. There's a spot about a quarter-mile ahead where we can turn around. Since we're going up a hill, take the reins and slap them once. These are good horses; they'll start pulling. As soon as they do, you release the brake. If you release it before they start pulling, the stage will roll backwards. Then the team would have to stop the backward roll of the stage before they can start pulling it forward."

Brad slapped the reins, the horses started pulling, and he released the brake. "It worked!" he exclaimed. "I'm driving the stage."

"The turn-around is just ahead." Jim pointed with his good arm. "Slowly pull back on the reins till the horses are walking. That's good. Now gently pull the reins to the right until we're well off the road. Good. Now to the left, and we'll circle around and head back down the hill toward Riverton. There's a way station a few miles back where can stop for help."

Audrey looked at the driver. His eyes were closed and his face was pale. "We'll be at the station in a little bit," she said encouragingly.

Audrey had her left arm behind the Mr. Bates and held onto the baggage rail. Her right hand gripped his right arm, helping him to sit up as he gave instructions to Brad.

"I see the way station," said Brad. "I'll pull back on the reins and press the brake with my foot."

"Don't press the brake too hard," he said. "It's okay to let the horses walk a little."

Brad walked the team to the front of the way station and then stopped the stage.

"Jim!" exclaimed Brennan O'Neil, running to the stage. "You're hurt! Let's get you inside and check you out. What happened?"

As they helped him down, Audrey told Mr. O'Neil about the holdup and why the driver was shot.

"That must have been Duke Badger. Your father told me about his gang."

"It was," said Brad. "One of his men called him Duke. Pa had a copy of the *Denver Post* in his office which had a story about him."

Mrs. O'Neil cleared a table and rolled a blanket to put under Jim's head. Brad and Mr. O'Neil helped Jim lie down on the table.

"Good bandaging," said Mrs. O'Neil removing the bandage. "Who did it?"

"Brad did," said Audrey as she nodded toward her brother. "He's good at it. He bandaged my arm this summer. Mrs. Adams told me that he'd done a good job."

"Well done," said Mrs. O'Neil.

"Thanks," said Brad. "Can you help him?"

"I'm not a doctor, Brad. You've done what I could do. If this was an emergency, I could probe for the bullet. However, Doc Adams is only four hours away. I'll do some more wrapping for the stage ride, but you should take him to Doc Adams. He can remove the slug and fix him up right. Let's get him back on the stage so you can get going to Riverton."

"Brad's a pretty good driver," said Mr. Bates. "He handles the team well, so I think we'll manage."

"Well, since he's a good driver, you're helping him, and I've only got one arm," said Brennan O'Neil, "there's no need for me to come along."

"Let's get you back on the stage and to Doc Adams," said Brad.

"Here's a canteen of water, Jim," said Mrs. O'Neil, "and here's some laudanum for the pain if you need it."

Brad helped Mr. Bates back into the driver's seat. The three elderly passengers agreed to ride with Brad driving, so Brennan O'Neil helped them re-board the stage.

Audrey climbed up into the seat beside Brad and Jim Bates. "The passengers are in, and the doors are closed, even the door with the hole. Let's go."

Brad released the brake and slapped the reins. The horses immediately started forward.

"Let 'em set the pace," Mr. Bates instructed. "They're an experienced team. The lead horse sets the pace, and the others follow. When you approach a sharp turn or a steep hill, pull back on the reins a little, and they'll slow down."

The jarring ride of the stage caused him to grimace in pain. After about fifteen minutes, he pulled out the bottle of laudanum, put it to his lips, and took a swallow.

"The pain's getting worse?" asked Brad.

"Yes, but I can only take little of this stuff. If I take too much, I'll fall asleep. Then I won't be able to help you."

"As soon as we get back, we'll send a wire to the Denver office," said Brad.

"What are we going to do about Pa?" asked Audrey. "We've got to help find him!"

"I'm worried too," said Brad. "Mr. Bates' wound is still bleeding, and riding on this stage aggravates it. Pa taught us how to bandage, but we're not doctors."

"Both of you are doing fine," he said. "Your father would be right proud of you if he knew what you're doing. You've probably saved my life with your bandaging, and there's no way I could drive this stage alone."

"Thanks, Mr. Bates," said Audrey.

"I'm starting to get a feel for the team and stage," said Brad, "but I'm really worried about Pa. I know Audrey is, too."

"Your Pa's a smart man. He's come out of bad situations before, and he'll come out of this one too."

"I want to believe that," said Audrey, "but I'm still afraid. Duke Badger's a nasty, mean, and evil man."

"Yes, he is an evil man," replied Jim. "But your father's a remarkable man. He's told me some real hair-raisers about the Civil War; they make this look like a church social."

"Pa told you about his battles in the Civil War?" questioned Brad.

"He fought in the war, same as other men, like Jake Jackson and Tom Shadden."

"But Tom was in the Confederate Army," said Audrey. "Pa was in the Union."

"True," he replied, "but there's a bond between soldiers, even when they fight on different sides, especially after a war."

"Pa was in worse situations than this?" asked Brad. "He's just been taken captive by a gang of outlaws."

"And the leader, Duke Badger, is an evil monster," said Audrey.

"Your father knows how to handle himself, and it looks like he's done a fine job preparing you for life as well. He takes you to church and sends you to school. He and Running Bear have taught both of you about the outdoors."

Brad thought about how Running Bear had trained them how to track and his recent teaming with them in the capture of the Big Foot gang.

"So this is kind of like a test," concluded Audrey.

"I don't mind tests at school," said Brad, "but I don't like tests that involve other people's lives."

Brad gently pulled back on the reins as the stage started down a hill. He looked at the trees and rocks and thought about his father. *Sheriff Tate won't be able to start searching for Pat until tomorrow morning. By the time the posse reaches the holdup site, it will be noon.*

Suddenly the right front wheel of the stage hit a

hole in the road. The wounded driver groaned from the painful jolt and uncorked the bottle of laudanum to take another swallow of the painkiller.

"There's the stream where we watered the horses this morning," said Brad. "I'll stop and rest the horses."

Audrey looked at Jim Bates and said, "You're getting mighty pale. You should ride inside."

Brad pulled back on the reins, and the horses slowed to a walk as they approached the shallow stream. After their two-hour run from the way station, they were ready for a rest and some water.

"I am feeling a might poorly. My head's spinning and I'm cold. I'd better get into the coach now, while I'm conscious and have the strength to walk."

Brad and Audrey helped him down from the driver's box and onto the floor of the stage. Audrey put her carpetbag under his head as a cushion.

"I know you don't feel like it, but you need to drink some water," said Audrey.

"We'll be in Riverton in a couple of hours," said Brad. "Mrs. Jones can hold your laudanum and canteen."

"I'll watch him real close, young feller. You just drive this stage so we can get him to a doctor," said Mrs. Jones.

"Come on Audrey, I may need your help," said her brother.

Brad and Audrey got back on the driver's bench. Brad released the brake, slapped the reins once, and the horses quickly returned to their previous pace.

"Brad, I'm scared. What if we never see Pa again? What if Mr. Bates dies?" said Audrey.

"I'm scared too! Pa is in the hands of that evil

man, but," Brad paused, "we mustn't let Duke Badger decide what's going to happen. We have to take charge. Reverend Wesley calls Duke Badger an evil monster, and now we know why. I don't know how, but we've got to save Mr. Bates and find Pa. We can't let Duke Badger win."

"Brad, I've never heard you sound so angry," said Audrey.

Brad gave his sister a puzzled look, thought for a moment, and replied, "I guess you're right; I am angry. Right now, we're doing everything we can for Mr. Bates. Let's think about how we can find Pa."

"I'd like to talk to Reverend Wesley and find out more about Duke Badger," said Audrey. "Sheriff Tate talked as if the reverend had met Duke at one time."

"Yes, let's talk to Reverend Wesley and Zeke, who was a member of the Big Foot Gang. Sheriff Tate told us about Zeke being on the work detail with Lutz Hall of the Badger Gang."

"It was some of Duke's gang that freed Lutz from the work detail," said Audrey.

"Before we go to bed tonight, come to my room so we can talk about Pa, Running Bear, and the holdup," said her brother.

"You think what Pa and Running Bear have taught us will help?" asked Audrey.

"Yes."

They rode in silence, thinking about what had happened and what they might do about it. A few minutes later, Audrey looked at Brad and said, "I'm going to ask how Mr. Bates is doing."

Audrey tightly gripped the baggage rail on top of the coach, hit the roof, and shouted, "How is Mr. Bates?"

"I gave him some more laudanum," replied Mrs. Jones. "He's pretty pale, but we're praying for him. You tell that young feller up there to keep driving. We're going to come out of this holdup fit as a fiddle."

The shadows of the trees got longer as the sun descended in the western sky. It was late afternoon, and the pace of the horses was slower by the time they reached the outskirts of Riverton.

"Riverton's only about a mile away," said Brad. "Remember, he's going to recover and Pa's going to come home."

"We're not going to let that...that evil monster ruin our lives," spat Audrey. "We're going to make Ma, Pa, and Running Bear proud of us."

"You bet," agreed Brad. "We're going to get our Pa back."

Brad pulled back ever so slightly on the reins and the horses slowed as they entered Riverton. As they approached the doctor's office, Brad pulled back harder on the reins and shouted "Whoa." Then he stepped on the brake, stopping the stage in front of Doc Adams' office. Sheriff Tate came out of his office next door and looked up to see Brad and Audrey in the driver's seat.

"Mr. Bates is inside; he's been shot!" exclaimed Audrey, seeing the sheriff.

"And Pa's been taken captive by the Badger Gang," added Brad.

"I'll go tell Doc Adams that we're bringing Mr. Bates up," said Audrey as she climbed down from the stage.

"Brad," ordered the sheriff, "get a couple of men to help me move Jim."

"Right away," replied Brad.

The sheriff opened the shattered stage door, saw Jim on the floor, and said, "Jim, can you hear me?"

"Yes," he groaned.

"This is Sheriff Tate. You're in Riverton and we're going to take you in to Doc Adams. Brad's getting a couple of men to help move you. He'll be back in just a minute."

Christopher Schmitt and Hans Finster came running up to the stage.

"Brad told us what happened," said Christopher. "Hans and I can help you. I brought a stretcher that I just finished making for the doctor."

"We can certainly use that," said the sheriff. "Christopher, you and Hans stay here. Brad and I'll go to the other side of the stage."

They placed stretcher beside Jim, and Sheriff Tate and Brad slid him onto it. Hans and Christopher then pulled the stretcher slowly out of the stage. Brad and Sheriff Tate each took a handle, and the four of them carried Jim up the steps into the doctor's office.

"Audrey, what in tarnation are you doin' on that stage?" asked Jake Jackson.

"I'm getting the baggage down, Mr. Jackson. Will you please help me? Brad and Sheriff Tate have just taken Mr. Bates to the doctor's office." Audrey told Jake about the holdup, Mr. Bates being shot, and her father being taken by the Badger Gang.

"Just throw those bags to me an I'll stack 'em," he said. "Then I'll get the bags from the boot."

While Jake Jackson got the bags from the baggage boot, Audrey gave them to their owners. When the baggage was all handed out, Jake came around and looked at the door to the stage.

"Them double barrels really make a hole," he said, poking his head through the hole in the door. "I'll take the stage to the corral. Tell the sheriff I'm taking care of the horses."

Jake climbed into the driver's seat, slapped the reins, and headed off. Audrey placed Brad's, her father's, and her own bags inside the sheriff's office. Then she climbed the steps to the doctor's office.

"The slug was pretty deep, and he lost a lot of blood," said the doctor. "Let's put him on the bed in the other room; I'll stay with him tonight."

The men picked up the stretcher, carried Jim into the other room, and gently placed him on the bed. Rosemary, Doc Adams' wife, tucked some blankets around Jim as the men left the room and closed the door.

"I didn't want to say this while he could hear me," said the doctor, "but I don't think he's going to make it. He's lost a lot of blood, and he's still in shock. Rosemary will bring him some soup in awhile. If we can get him to eat something and keep him warm, and the Lord is willing, he might live."

They heard the sound of someone climbing the stairs. Doc Adams stopped talking, and everyone looked at the door as Reverend Wesley entered the doctor's office.

"I just heard about Jim," said the reverend. "How is he, Doc?"

Doc Adams told the reverend about Jim's condition

and then said, "He needs your help now, Reverend. I've done everything I can."

Reverend Wesley opened the door to the back room and entered.

Mrs. Adams sat in a chair beside the bed, holding Jim's right hand. "I'll be back in a while with some soup, Jim. Reverend Wesley is here to see you." She left the room, and Reverend Wesley sat down beside Jim.

Several minutes later, Brad, Audrey, and the others looked up as the reverend gently closed the door to the back room. "Ladies, men, let us bow our heads," said Reverend Wesley. "Lord, Jim's been hurt, and he needs your help. He was shot by Duke Badger, an evil man."

The sound of a horse pulling a buckboard came through the open window. The reverend continued, ending his prayer with, "Jim is a good man. We need him; you need him in our never-ending war with evil. We ask you to please spare his life and let him continue serving you in Riverton. This we ask in the name of your son, Jesus Christ. Amen."

Audrey wiped a tear from her face as Brad put his arm around her. "We've got to send a telegram to Denver," he said to her quietly.

Reverend Wesley looked around and said, "Let's go home and keep Jim Bates and Harold Benton in our thoughts. Pray for them tonight and every night."

"We'll see you Sunday," said Sheriff Tate leaving the room.

"See you Sunday," said Hans Finster, following Christopher Schmitt and the sheriff out the door.

Brad and Audrey went down the steps and saw Jake

Jackson standing beside a buckboard. "I thought you young'uns' could use a ride home," he said.

"We sure could," said Brad. "Can we stop by the depot first? We need to send a telegram to Denver."

"Sure," Jake replied. "Don't worry about your bags; I already got 'em from the sheriff's office. Hop on, and we'll head over to the depot."

"Thanks," said Brad.

Brad and Audrey climbed on the buckboard, and Mr. Jackson headed to the depot.

"Real shame 'bout your Pa," he said. "Sheriff Tate's gittin' a posse together first thing in the mornin'; Duke Badger's just plain nasty."

"When the strongbox didn't have any gold, he took Mr. Bates' shotgun and blew a hole in the door. Then he smashed the shotgun on the wheel of the stage," said Audrey.

"He's got a temper all right," replied Jake. "Here's the depot. Who ya' sendin' the wire to?"

"The Overland Stage office in Denver," replied Brad. "Let's go, Audrey."

Brad and Audrey entered the telegraph office and were greeted by Mr. Donatelli. "Good afternoon, Mr. Donatelli. We need to send a telegram to Denver," announced Brad.

Mr. Donatelli's dark hair, dark eyes, and olive skin showed his Italian heritage. He and his wife, Gina, had come to Riverton ten years earlier. They had two children; Arturo was in the fourth grade, and Enrico was in the third grade.

"Sure, Brad. Is it for your father?"

"Well, it's for the business," said Brad. He explained about the holdup and his father being taken captive.

"I'm sorry about your father. I'll charge it to the Overland account. I'm sure the outlaws dropped him off after a few miles. He's probably made it to the way station by now," said Mr. Donatelli.

Brad and Audrey wrote the message:

Wednesday, 20 October, stage robbed one mile north of Riverton way station. STOP. Driver Jim Bates shot, may not live. STOP. Harold Benton taken captive by Badger Gang. STOP. Brad Benton drove stage with wounded driver back to Riverton. STOP. Brad and Audrey Benton sending. STOP.

"Here's the message, Mr. Donatelli," said Brad. "We've got to go now; Mr. Jackson is driving us home. We'll come back tomorrow."

Brad put his arm around his sister as they rode the buckboard home. Tears ran down Audrey's face, and Brad had a lump in his throat when they stopped under the oak tree in their front yard.

"You've had a tough day," said Jake Jackson. "Let's git ya' inside and tell your Ma and Grandma about the holdup."

Hearing the buckboard, Mrs. Benton and their grandmother, Victoria, came to the front door.

"Brad! Audrey!" exclaimed their mother. "What are you doing back here?"

"There was a holdup north of the Riverton way

station. Duke Badger shot Mr. Bates and took Pa," explained Brad as he and Audrey jumped from the buckboard and rushed to their mother. "Mr. Bates is at Doc Adam's office; he may not live."

Abby Benton hugged her children. "Thank you for bringing my children home, Jake," she said fighting back tears. Victoria put her arm around Abby.

Jake tipped his hat and said, "Least I could do, Mrs. Benton. Your husband would be right proud of Brad and Audrey. They bandaged Jim; saved his life. Brad drove the stage all the way back ta' Riverton. They just sent a wire to Denver 'bout the holdup."

"Ma," cried Audrey, "we did everything Duke Badger told us to do, but he still shot Mr. Bates and took Pa!"

"We got Mr. Bates bandaged up," continued Brad, his voice quivering. "He taught me how to drive the stage, but then we had to put him inside before he passed out."

"If ya' need anything Mrs. Benton, just holler, and I'll come help ya'," offered Jake.

"We will," said Victoria, "and thank you."

"Someone's coming," said Brad, pointing to a rider heading toward the house.

"It's Sheriff Tate," said Abby.

The sheriff halted his horse by the buckboard, dismounted, and walked over to the Bentons.

"Evening, Richard," said Abby.

"Evening, Abby," replied Sheriff Tate, tipping his hat. "I came to tell you that fifteen men have volunteered for the posse. We'll be leaving first thing in the morning. I wired Sheriff Strong in Denver and asked him to notify the Army. If they have the manpower, they'll send a patrol to help search for your Harold."

"Thank you Richard; I know you'll do your best," said Abby.

"I thought you should know that Brad and Audrey did a first-rate job of bandaging Jim. Doc Adams said he couldn't have done better." Sheriff Tate lowered his eyes and coughed.

"You've got something else to say, Richard," observed Victoria. "Go ahead and say it."

"Well, Doc Adams said Jim is pretty bad. He's not sure he'll live through the night. Brad, Audrey, you did everything you could for him. You should be proud."

"We'll pray for him," said Victoria.

"Good night, Richard. Thanks for stopping by," said Abby Benton.

"I'll ride back to town with ya'," offered Jake.

"See you when we come back," said Sheriff Tate. "Good night Abby, Victoria, Audrey, Brad."

The sheriff mounted his horse and headed back to town at a trot. Jake slapped the reins and followed him in the buckboard.

"Ready to talk?" asked Audrey.

Brad looked at his sister standing in the doorway to his room and nodded. Audrey entered and closed the door. Brad sat on the floor leaning back against his bed, and Audrey plopped down across from him, her back against the wall.

"Remember when we went camping with Pa just before school started?" asked Brad.

192

"Of course, how could I forget? You shot your new rifle, and we had roast pheasant, baked potatoes, and lemonade for supper. Pa helped us polish our shooting skills; we blasted all those pinecones on that old log. He even taught us how to make a shelter, just in case we're ever in a situation where we need one."

"That was a good pheasant dinner," said Brad. "Your pancakes the next morning were great, too."

"Pa said they sure could have used pancakes like mine when he was in the army," she replied, a smile coming to her face.

Brad gazed out his bedroom window at the last rays of sunshine glinting off the barn. Audrey pulled her knees up, wrapped her arms around them, and looked at her brother. Brad slowly turned his head from the window and back to his sister a moment before speaking.

"If Sheriff Tate doesn't find Pa, will you go with me to hunt for him?" he asked, leaning forward.

Audrey closed her eyes, silently pondering his question. His question was like a distant bolt of lightning. Brad waited patiently for his sister's response. She finally opened her eyes and answered softly, like a muffled clap of thunder replying to her brother's lightning bolt.

"Yes," she whispered, barely audible whisper. "Yes, I'll go with you."

"I knew you would, but I had to ask," he said, slumping back against his bed. "Mr. Bates said that this is one of life's tests. Pa and Running Bear have taught us everything we need to know. We can both shoot accurately, and we know how to ride. Ebony and Blaze are good horses. We know how to cook, how to treat wounds, and how to build a shelter. We even know how to live off the land if necessary."

"Harvest vacation wasn't supposed to be like this," said Audrey. "They closed the school for two weeks so the children could help harvest the crops. Just think what might have happened if we had stayed to help with the harvest instead of going to Denver with Pa. I was hoping to get some music for Ma."

"And I was supposed to get some things for Nana," said Brad.

"We won't get to do those things this year," said Audrey.

"No," replied her brother, "but I'm glad Ma is teaching that class at Riverton Bible College during the vacation," said Brad.

"Yes," agreed his sister. "Thank goodness she wasn't on the stage. I still have the list of things to get in Denver," she said, pulling it out of her pocket.

Brad touched his shirt pocket. "I have my list too."

"Sheriff Tate and the posse should be back by Saturday," said Audrey. "Let's get some sleep; we've got to talk to Reverend Wesley tomorrow."

"Sure," said Brad, standing up and opening the door for his sister. "See you in the morning."

"Good night, Brad," said Audrey. "And thank you for asking me to help you. If you hadn't, I would have asked you to join me in hunting for Pa!"

OTHER TITLES BY THIS AUTHOR

THE BIGFOOT GANG

CAPTIVE

FIERY BLIZZARD

ABOUT THE AUTHOR

Born and raised in the West, Smith grew up where many farmers still used horses to plow their fields. Steam engines were the norm for railroads, and a diesel locomotive was quite an event. He's now caught up with civilization. After a tour with the Air Force, teaching, musician, government employee, he's settled down and lives in Virginia. You can find out more about him at www.edgsmith.com.

CONNECT WITH THE AUTHOR

Website:
www.edgsmith.com

Social Media:
www.facebook.com/edgsmith

ACKNOWLEDGEMENTS:

Many thanks to Liza for enhancing clarity, editing for all that grammar stuff, and partnering with me to bring the Benton Series to fruition. And to her daughter, Lauren, for the young adult assessment. A special atta-girl for Susie Nunez's special skills in making the liner comments {jacket items (author bio, about paragraph) cover description} come alive.